The GLUE

a taboo treat

Mandy,
Lox3!
♡ K~~~~~

K WEBSTER

The Glue
Copyright © 2018 K Webster

ISBN-13:978-1726337052
ISBN-10:1726337057

Cover Design: All By Design
Photo: Adobe Stock
Editor: Emily A. Lawrence,
www.lawrenceediting.com
Formatting: Champagne Book Design

I'm a fixer. A lover. Always searching for the right fit.
And I come up empty every time.
My desires are unusual.
I don't feel whole until I'm in the middle, holding it all together.
Which makes having a romantic relationship really difficult.

Until them.
Two people. An unraveling marriage. Love on the rocks.
And they want me.
To put them back together again.

Problem is, once they're fixed, where does that leave me?
I sure as hell hope I stick like glue.

PLAYLIST

Listen on Spotify

"Jealous Sea" by Meg Myers
"The Death of Me" by Meg Myers
"Devour" by Marilyn Manson
"Blown Wide Open" by Big Wreck
"Hold Me Down" by Halsey
"Can You Hold Me" by NF
"How's It Going To Be" by Third Eye Blind
"I Found" by Amber Run
"Codex" by Radiohead
"Lonely Boy" by The Black Keys
"Way Down We Go" by Kaleo
"Desire" by Meg Myers
"Where Is My Mind" by Pixies
"Crawl" by Kings of Leon
"Tainted Love" by Marilyn Manson
"Glory And Gore" by Lorde
"Oh My" by Big Wreck
"Glycerine" by Bush
"Meet On The Ledge" by Greta Van Fleet
"The Night We Met" by Lord Huron
"Dark Side" by Bishop Briggs

"#1 Crush" by Garbage
"In The Meantime" by Spacehog
"Uprising" by Muse
"Closer" by Nine Inch Nails
"The Beautiful People" by Marilyn Manson
"Uninvited" by Alanis Morissette
"Wrecking Ball" by Miley Cyrus
"Blurred Lines" by Robin Thicke, T.I., & Pharrell Williams
"River" by Bishop Briggs
"I'll Be Missing You (feat. 112)" by Diddy, Faith Evans, & 112
"Two Princes" by Spin Doctors
"Bitter Sweet Symphony" by The Verve
"Linger" by The Cranberries
"Don't Look Back in Anger" by Oasis

DEDICATION

To Matt—I'm stuck on you like glue.
How's that for a corny dedication?
You're welcome, honey.

the
GLUE

a taboo treat

"True love stories never have endings."

—Richard Bach

K Webster's Taboo World

Welcome to my taboo world! These stories began as an effort to satisfy the taboo cravings in my reader group. The two stories in the duet, *Bad Bad Bad*, were written off the cuff and on the fly for my group. Since everyone seemed to love the stories so much, I expanded the characters and the world. I've been adding new stories ever since. Each book stands alone from the others and doesn't need to be read in any particular order. I hope you enjoy the naughty characters in this town! These are quick reads sure to satisfy your craving for instalove, smokin' hot sex, and happily ever afters!

Bad Bad Bad
Coach Long
Ex-Rated Attraction
Mr. Blakely
Malfeasance
Easton
Crybaby
Lawn Boys
Renner's Rules
The Glue

Several more titles to be released soon!
Thanks for reading!
K

Chapter
ONE

Aiden

He's finally proposed. Such a revelation should bring a smile to my face, but I can't stop glaring at my phone. Bitter at my twin brother, Anthony's, happiness. Something I never thought would happen.

God, I'm such a dick.

With a sigh, I fire off my reply.

Me: Congrats, man. Send Steph my love.

His reply is immediate.

Ugly Twin: Come by the house and have dinner with us. We don't fucking see you anymore.

I'm just about to reply when a deep, husky voice stops me.

"Is macroeconomics so boring to you that you'd rather text your friends than take notes that'll be on the first exam next week?"

Gritting my teeth, I shove my phone into my hoodie pocket and meet the hard, unrelenting glare of Professor Young, who's standing in front of my table.

"Carry on," I mutter, hating the way the entire classroom of nearly a hundred students all turn to watch me. They snigger and smirk, happy for the distraction.

Professor Young's black brows furl together as if I've angered him by my response. I just want him to go away. Back to the front of the classroom where I can appreciate his perfect ass in his charcoal-gray slacks from afar. Always from afar.

"See me after class," he bites out, irritation in his tone.

I give him a clipped nod. He turns on his heel and stalks down the steps toward the front of the classroom. With each step, the fabric grips the back of his thighs, accentuating his firm ass. My cock stirs in my jeans and I stifle a groan. Of course I'd be into Professor Jerkoff.

But assholes are my MO after all.

My last relationship ended fucking terribly last month. And the one before even worse. I've tasted pussy and sucked cock. Just when I think I'm over one—in this case, men—I get a hard-on from this hot professor's ass. A man. It's like my brain can't make up its fucking mind.

I love tits, dammit.

My dick jolts in agreement.

But all it takes is watching some gay porn on Tumblr and I'm all kinds of confused again.

Crack!

I jerk my attention to the board where Professor Jerkoff holds a ruler and points to something he's written and circled. His light brown eyes narrow as he gives me a warning glare. Two classes with this guy and I'm already thinking I'm going to have to drop. No damn way I can take this for an entire semester.

The class goes by in a fog and I struggle to focus. My mind keeps flitting back to Anthony's *fiancée*, Steph. She was the first woman I'd gone down on. The first person I'd ever done anything sexually with. It was all fun and games until my twin staked his claim.

And now she's marrying my brother.

I knew they were in love and I knew he'd bought her a ring to propose with, but I just honestly didn't expect him to follow through with it. Everything about their relationship went so quickly.

The thought of Dad's reaction when he finds out

has me stifling a chuckle. Our father likes control. When Anthony started seeing Stephanie, a woman closer to Dad's age rather than ours, he'd about blown a gasket. It took some getting used to, but now everything is hunky-fucking-dory.

Chairs start scraping and it's then I realize everyone is leaving. I lift my gaze and wonder if I can slip out past Professor Jerkoff. His piercing stare has me pinned. There's no escape.

"Mr. Blakely," he calls out, his tone sharp. It's as though he knows I'm ready to bail.

I grab my backpack and throw it over my shoulder. I have one semester of college under my belt and I already fucking hate it. I'm not like Anthony. I don't desire to grow up and take over Dad's advertising firm. I'm not sure what I want to do, but it's certainly not that.

Avoiding my professor's glare, I stare at my black Vans as I clomp noisily down the stairs. The classroom quickly leaves, so by the time I reach the bottom, we're the only two people left.

"Macroeconomics is a requirement," he says coolly.

"Yep."

"You meet someone's eyes when you're spoken

to," he snaps.

My head jerks up. He glowers at me, a vein in his neck throbbing out of control. Heat skates across my flesh and settles on my neck at the thought of running my tongue along that vein. Fuck, why does he have to be so damn good-looking?

His features soften and he crosses his sculpted arms over his chest. I appreciate the male form. This man is a beautiful work of art.

"You're not dropping out," he states in a matter-of-fact tone.

My jaw drops in shock. "W-What? Why not?"

"Like I said. It's a requirement. Econ doesn't simply go away. It doesn't get any easier. And I can guarantee you that you won't find a better teacher than myself." His tone is smug.

"I'll take my chances," I mutter.

"No. You won't."

We have a heated staring match until I glance over at the clock. "I have to get to my job."

He studies me for a moment. "I need a TA."

I almost laugh at his joke until I realize he's serious. "Wait. You're suggesting I be your teacher's assistant? You don't even like me." I gesture for the board. "I'm not even good at this shit."

The corners of his lips twitch with amusement and fuck if it doesn't affect me. My cock likes this asshole a hell of a lot more than I do. "Which is why you'll make a lovely assistant. You need me and I need you. Help me grade papers and respond to online queries from students, and I'll make sure you pass this class." He points to a seat right in the front row. "And that's where you'll sit. Where I can keep my eyes on you."

Heat flickers in his stare and I'm confused for a moment. Is my professor hitting on me? I'm not confident enough that he's hitting on me to flirt back so I simply shrug my shoulders.

"I'll probably disappoint you." God knows Dad is disappointed. I've already got more lectures than I can count and college has barely started. If it weren't for my stepmom, I'd probably just move out. She comes to my defense every time and makes him back off.

"I highly doubt that," he replies, a smile tugging at his lips.

I rub at the back of my neck and avoid his hot look. I'm not sure if I'm reading more into things or if this dude is being more than friendly. He's not wearing a ring, but I don't know much about him. Maybe he's into guys. Dad would really have a shitfit if I had sex with my professor.

The thought of Professor Young with his shirt off and his pants undone is enough to have me suppressing a groan. My cock is hard in my jeans and I need to get the hell out of here before I embarrass myself any further.

"Great, see you around," I mutter as I bolt and don't bother turning around.

The bell above the door jingles as I enter the cute coffee shop after class. I'm starting my job at Java Jive today and am actually looking forward to it. While school is boring, I enjoy work. For years, I worked at a bakery here in town, but I had to quit after an argument with my boss. I'm ready to get out of the house and make some money again. There's nothing more emasculating than having to ask your dad for cash.

"I'll be right there!" a female's voice calls out, cheerful and musical in quality.

I smile and look around the space. It's completely empty. The décor is feminine and florally—not really fitting for a coffee shop. All distaste for the décor flies out the window, though, when I get a whiff of something delicious. I walk over to the glass display case and notice many desserts inside. Having not eaten all day, my stomach grumbles. I'm just glancing over the menu when the door to the back flies open and someone rushes out.

The first thing I notice are the widest, greenest, most innocent eyes I've ever seen. I'm struck by how they look like two glimmering gems you'd see dangling from a pair of earrings. A quick perusal and I see the woman has high cheekbones that are splotching pink as if she's been exerting herself. Her nose is small and slightly upturned. A sprinkle of freckles hides beneath a smudge of flour on her flesh.

But her lips…

Goddamn, those lips.

Full and succulent. The kind of lips most women pay money to have, but these are all natural.

"Can I help you?" she squeaks out, her voice slightly hoarse as if she's embarrassed.

I meet her eyes again and her cheeks blaze even redder. I can't help but grin at her. She's fucking gorgeous. A tendril of silky reddish-brown hair falls into her face and she blows it away only for it to fall right back into her eyes.

"I'm Aiden," I tell her, my smile growing wider.

"Vale. Nice you meet you."

My smile falls. "You're the Vale I spoke to on the phone. As in you own this coffee shop?"

Finally, she smiles at me and it lights up the small shop. Her two front teeth are slightly bigger than the rest, but it gives her character. So fucking cute. I can't believe my soon-to-be boss is the prettiest woman I've ever laid eyes on.

"You're Aiden Blakely?" she breathes out in astonishment. "My employee?"

"If you'll have me," I tease. I can't help but flirt with her. Where flirting—unlike my twin who's a natural at it—doesn't usually come easy for me, with Vale, it is easy. Boss or not, I'm going to get to know this woman better. Her mouth was made for sucking and adoring.

"I need you," she says with a sigh.

Silence falls between us and her throat turns bright red. She bites on her fat bottom lip and stares helplessly at me.

"I need you too." My voice is husky and filled with insinuation.

"W-With the shop," she whispers, clarifying her words. "I need your help so I don't have to close it."

I study her features. She's nervous and unsure but sweet. I like her instantly. Working with her would be the highlight of my boring-ass day.

"What have you been making?" I brush my thumb across my nose to indicate she has flour there. "Smells good."

Her nervousness fades and her smile brightens. "Chocolate chunk cookies with lavender. Sounds gross, huh? But would you believe they taste sooooo good?" She pats her stomach over her apron. "They've barely come out of the oven and I've had three." Her shoulders lift up as she shrugs.

"So this is a bakery?" I point to the display case. "I thought you were a coffee shop."

Her lips press together and her auburn brows crush together. "It was at first. Then, I started baking more. Nobody drinks the coffee here anyway," she says with a pout. "Something has to change or I'll be forced to close it down."

"It sounds like your shop needs a facelift. Maybe some remarketing and a new business plan." Okay, so maybe I am just like Dad. "But first, I better taste those cookies to make sure they're as good as you say they are."

She laughs and the sound makes my chest ache. I want to make her do that a heck of a lot more.

"Come back here, wise guy. You'll love them.

Trust me." She winks at me before disappearing into the back.

I walk behind the counter and follow her into the kitchen. Trays of cookies line the tables and it smells even more heavenly. With her back to me, I inspect her without shame. She's a good head shorter than my six-foot-three frame. The black leggings she's wearing are glued to her curvy thighs and ass like a second skin. She wears tan-colored boots that go to her knees and a mauve top that is silky.

That ass, though.

For the second time today, my cock is wide fucking awake. Just like with Professor Jerkoff, I'm attracted to this person. Maybe I just need to get laid because right now everyone I come in contact with looks good enough to fuck.

"Here." She holds out a giant cookie in her gloved hand.

Instead of taking the cookie, I lean forward and take a bite. Her glowing green eyes widen at my bold move. Our faces are just inches apart. I can smell the sweetness of the cookie, but I get a whiff of her floral perfume and it makes me want to bury my face in her hair to inhale her.

I pull slightly away and chew, my eyes glued to

hers. She blinks rapidly and gives me a close-lipped smile. It makes me want to say something funny so she'll grin at me again with her imperfect smile that I could stare at for days. Once I swallow, I step back and pin her with a serious look.

"You need to rebrand right away. I can get my dad's help, but if all your baked treats are as good as this, then you need to be focusing on that. Your coffee and grandma décor aren't pulling the customers in, so what do you have to lose?"

She scrunches her flour-dusted freckled nose at me. "I hired you to pour coffee and take money so I could work on marketing."

I reach forward and take the cookie from her hand, letting my own hand brush against her smaller one. "Well, until the customers are lined up at the door to buy your coffee, I'll help you with the new marketing plan."

She once again blows on her hair. "You're just going to swoop in and save the day, huh?" Her hair falls back in her face. I love how seemingly messy she is. Slightly frazzled. It's adorable.

I lean forward and brush her hair from her face and tuck it behind her ear, enjoying the way her skin turns bright red at my touch. Her body is so receptive.

Makes me eager to get to know it better. I wonder how red I can get her pale flesh with my mouth.

"I'm going to save the day," I agree, my voice low as I stare at her plump lips. "If you'll let me."

Her lashes flutter against her cheeks. "I want you. I'll let you." Her words are breathless.

Smiling, I swipe the flour off her nose. "Then I will." I drop my gaze to her mouth again and lick my lips. "I'll do it now that you've agreed to it."

Our eyes meet and hers are hot with understanding.

We're not simply talking about a job here.

We're talking about everything.

Chapter
TWO

Aiden

"How's the new job going?" Dad calls out as I walk past his office.

I stop and peek my head inside. "I love it."

His features are normally hard and stoic, but my stepmother softens him in all the right ways. The corners of his eyes crinkle as he smiles at me. Dad doesn't smile too much, but when he does, I see myself in him. "A barista, huh?"

I lean my shoulder against the doorframe and grin. "Barista slash baker slash marketing extraordinaire." I've gone into Vale's coffee shop two afternoons in a row. This afternoon, after my third class with Professor Jerkoff, it will make a third afternoon in a row. Spending all evenings watching Vale bend over and grab things from lower shelves is the highlight of my day. The woman has the most perfect curvy ass. She put me to work right away and was shocked at my ability in a kitchen. I think it made her more excited because she stopped acting nervous and after two days, talks my ear off. I flirt with her nonstop and she flirts too. "It's a great job."

Dad lifts a dark brow as he scrutinizes me. "Who is she?"

I rub at the back of my neck and shrug. "Who?"

"The girl who has you all up in knots. Who's the girl?" His steel-blue eyes that match my own twinkle with pride. "Better yet, when do we get to meet her?"

Laughing, I shake my head at him. "Whoa, man, you can stop writing out the wedding invitations. She's just beautiful and funny and sweet. I'm trying to get to know her right now. Not pushing anything."

He gives me a knowing smirk. "You know Ava is going to go crazy the moment she finds out you like someone. Just warning you. Be prepared to bring her to dinner the minute you've gotten to know her."

"Got it."

I slip out of the house and stride out to Dad's old Lexus. He got a new Land Rover recently and gave me his old car. It's still badass and I don't have to make payments on it, so I'm happy. I'm just climbing inside when my phone rings. I don't recognize the number.

"Hello?"

"Mr. Blakely."

A beat of silence.

Heat rushes up my spine and warms my flesh. "What's up, Mr. Young?" How in the hell does Professor Jerkoff have my phone number?

"We need to meet up so I can discuss what I need help with. Are you free today?"

"I'm headed to work, but I'll be off around eight."

"I'll be on campus still. Come to my office after work," he instructs, his deep voice gravelly and bossy as fuck.

I can't even lie that it doesn't get my dick hard.

"Got it."

"Okay then," he grunts.

Click.

No bye. Nothing. Fuck, he's such an asshole.

I turn the engine over and speed out of our neighborhood. At least Vale is fucking nice. Spending time with her is awesome. I'm lost in thoughts of her tight leggings and pouty lips that the drive goes by in a flash. When I pull up out front, I'm the only car in front of the building. The place looks sad as fuck. It's a shame.

Vale really is a good cook.

I get out and hurry inside. The bell chimes, but she doesn't holler from the back like usual. It bothers me that anyone could sneak inside here and get her. She's completely oblivious. I stalk to the back and find her sitting on a stool talking on the phone. Her bottom lip is wobbling as tears streak down her apple cheeks. Crossing my arms, I stare at her, waiting for her to get off the phone so I can lay into her for not being safe.

"Who is she?" she breathes, accusation in her tone.

Whomever she's talking to starts yelling on the other end and she tenses.

"Okay, I'm sorry," she mutters. "I know. It's fine. Forget I said anything." Then, she huffs. "Bye to you too."

She stuffs her phone in her apron and then jolts when she notices me standing there.

"Anyone could have walked in and taken advantage of you," I grumble, walking over to her.

She rolls her eyes and stands. "Don't you start too."

I clench my jaw but don't say any more on the matter. "Come here."

Surprisingly, she lets me pull her into my arms.

My giant body dwarfs hers, but it feels right. She hugs me tight and sniffles.

"Bad day?"

She laughs humorlessly. "Each day gets worse and worse."

"Want to talk about it?"

"No. I want to escape it." She tilts her head up and looks at me. Her plump, juicy lips part as her glittering green eyes regard me.

I could kiss her. I sure as hell want to. My dick is at attention and there's no doubt she doesn't notice. But I'm not like Anthony. He'd have her naked and fucking her against the freezer to cheer her up. I'm wired differently. I'd love nothing more than to fuck my new boss, but something tells me that won't help lift her spirits. Sure, maybe for those few blissful moments as she screamed my name. But then what?

We have to start with what I came here for.

I press a kiss to her forehead. "Let's talk shop then. I researched a bunch of shit in class today."

She laughs and her eyes sparkle with happiness. Yes, this is what I like seeing from this beautiful woman. Happiness I put there.

"Shouldn't you be paying attention?" she challenges with an arched brow.

"And let the coffee shop go under?" I ask in faux horror. "Absolutely not. Reviving this place is my new mission in life. I'm going to help you."

"Thank you," she says, grinning.

We spend the next few hours on my computer mapping out ideas and brainstorming. She helps all three of the customers who come in. Vale is a natural with people. It's too bad more people didn't get to meet her.

"Is there a reason why you have those hideous things?" I gesture to the gaudy curtains across the windows.

"Hideous?" she shrieks and runs over to them. She pets them and grins. "They're beautiful."

"Lies. They're horrible."

Her lips pout out, but I won't budge on this. "I made them."

Okay, so maybe I can budge.

I stand and walk over to her. The urge to touch her is strong. I settle for grabbing her hand to help soften the blow.

"This isn't 1997."

She gasps. "Asshole."

I smirk and squeeze her hand. "They have to go. Now."

She groans and complains as I stand on a chair to start pulling the curtains from their rods. Once they're all gone, I gesture to the windows.

"Now, they can see you." I walk over to her and stand close. I like her scent. "They need to see you."

Her head tilts up and she smiles. A blush creeps up her throat. An unruly lock of her hair falls across her eye. Gently, I raise my hand and brush it away before tucking it behind her ear. I let my palm linger and run my thumb across her jaw bone.

"Aiden," she breathes, her lips parting.

"You're the best thing about this place," I murmur, my gaze focused on her pouty lips. "They need to see you."

Our eyes meet again and hers are glassy. Whatever had her upset earlier today has her lip trembling and tears threatening. One leaks out and I swipe it away with my thumb.

"I'm going to help you fix things," I vow.

She swallows and nods. "I need the help. God, do I ever. I'm falling apart."

I open my mouth, but then her phone is ringing from the back. She pulls away as if waking from a dream and scurries off. When I glance at the clock, it's fifteen after eight.

Fuck.

I follow her to the back and she's arguing with someone on the phone. I toss her a wave and then I'm rushing to campus. It's nearly half past eight by the time I arrive. The parking lot is empty aside from a black Tahoe.

Not a great way to start my meeting off with Professor Jerkoff. I climb out of my car, ignoring the cold bite of the wind, and hustle to the building. It's warm inside and the halls are dark aside from light coming from an office down at the end of the hallway. I trot down to his office, ready to barge in, but stop short when I realize he's on the phone.

"Fuck, woman. Do you need proof? Seriously, it's ridiculous. I'll see you in an hour."

He slams his phone down on the desk and curses. His chair creaks and I bite back a groan. The last thing I want to do is deal with a doubly pissed off professor. I could slowly back away.

"You're late," he says coolly from inside his office.

Fuck.

No escaping now.

Chapter
THREE

Vaughn

He curses from the hallway and then appears in the doorway. My eyes, against their wishes, rake over his handsome appearance. His dark hair is messy and windblown. A rosy pink from the chilly air has colored his cheeks. And those lips.

Goddamn him.

Those lips are pouty as fuck. Apparently I have a thing for full, kissable lips. My downfall every time.

"Sit," I bark out harshly in an effort to hide his effect on me. I'm in no place to be getting aroused by a student. As if my life isn't complicated enough.

His brows furl together and his jaw clenches as though he barely holds back what he wants to say to me. I let my eyes roam over his clothes. A dark gray hoodie that fits his biceps a little snugly and dark, holey jeans. He wears the same black Vans I've seen him in each time. As he sits in the chair across from me, I adjust my semi erection discreetly and lean back in my seat. He scratches at the stubble on his cheek before pinning me with a smug half smile.

"Sorry. Got tied up at work." His blue eyes flicker as though the memory of work is more preferable than sitting with me. At least one of us enjoys his job.

"If you're going to be my TA, I need punctuality," I growl.

His eyes narrow. "Then you have the wrong guy."

Our eyes lock for a heated moment and I tug at the knot of my tie to loosen it. I need to get laid. Maybe this bullshit attraction to my male student will go the fuck away. I haven't felt physically drawn to another person—another male—since before I was married. Back then, I slept around with guys more often than women, so it was a little surprising to myself that I married a woman.

Married.

That is the big problem.

You're supposed to get married and only have eyes for one. You get to fuck your best friend whenever you want. People don't tell you that sometimes, your best friend gives up on you. Or that sometimes, you disappoint your best friend. They sure as fuck don't tell you that the very things that bring other couples together are what could drive mile-long wedges between your own relationship.

"Professor?"

I grit my teeth and shake away the thoughts of my crumbling marriage. My wife hates me. Sure as hell doesn't trust me. And we're about three arguments away from divorce. Which is why I'm feeling weak these past few days and letting my eyes wander to the man who oozes sex appeal and has made my office ten degrees warmer just by being in it.

Clearing my throat, I shake my head at him. "Call me Vaughn. At least when not in the classroom."

"Okay, *Vaughn*," Aiden says, his gravelly voice sending pulses of excitement straight to my dick. "What are we here to talk about?"

This office is too fucking hot. I jerk away my loosened tie, shoving it in my drawer. Then, I unbutton the top two buttons. Aiden's steely gaze is sharp and focused on my actions.

"I'll be giving you the test key, after you've taken your own tests of course, after each exam. I'll need those graded promptly and brought back to me the following day. As for the weekly assignments, I will want you to grade those as well. I'll be using my time preparing for my lectures. You'll be given a key to my office to come and go as you please to get what you need. I have a locked drawer you can put the graded assignments in. On certain occasions, I may need to meet up with you the night before so I can get them."

His brow arches. "Will there be a lot of evening meetings?"

Again, I adjust my annoyingly hard cock and drag my stare away from his hot one to the window. "Perhaps. I need you available."

"And I need you to remember I have a job I very much enjoy. A job I don't want to lose. As long as you understand my life doesn't revolve around helping you, I'm good," he grumbles.

"A temporary job. The whole point of college is to get a better job that makes more money," I snap back, irritation surging through me. "I'm doing you a favor. You get one-on-one help from me essentially whenever you need it and it looks good on your résumé."

He laughs. "You sound like my dad."

"If I were your dad, I would've whipped your ass for being a smart aleck."

His eyes widen and his nostrils flare. "Good thing

you're not my dad."

A groan rumbles from me and I run my fingers through my hair, ruining the gel. I'm tired and stressed the fuck out. And now I've crossed a line by cursing at my student and saying inappropriate things.

"I'm sorry," I hiss out. "I've just had a bad day."

"And I've had a good one," he says, his voice husky. "Until now."

I stand from my seat, no longer okay with being trapped behind my desk, and pace the small office. My cock is still aching in my slacks and presses against the fabric. When I sneak a look at him, he's fiddling with his shoe lace, not looking at me. I walk over to the window and stare out at the empty parking lot.

I used to be eager to send my last student from my office and then hurry to meet my wife for dinner. Now, I make up excuses to stay away. I can't handle the continuous tears. The anger. The constant look of disappointment in her eyes.

I'm good at a lot of things, but I've fucking failed her in so many ways.

Especially one.

Probably the most important one of all.

The chair creaks from behind me as he stands.

"If that's all, I'm going to head out. I need to get

home and study," he says.

I turn and he's standing too close. Just as tall as me. Lean and muscular. A handsome, youthful face. He's every bit like those Abercrombie models I see on the walls when my wife drags me into the store in the mall. Fuck if he doesn't smell like that store too.

"That's all. We'll be in touch," I grit out, my eyes falling to those kissable lips once more.

I would never cheat on my wife, but hell if I don't wonder what those lips taste like. As if clued into my thoughts, he licks them. His blue eyes blaze with intensity.

"See you around, Vaughn." He winks at me.

Then, he turns on his heel and saunters out of my office, leaving me with a full hard-on and disgust at myself running through my veins.

I pull up to our midtown bungalow nestled near downtown and park on the street. I watch my wife as she flits about in the kitchen. There's a pep in her step that reminds me of the beginning. Back when we were so fucking in love.

Now?

She hates me.

She hates everything I am and everything I'm not.

I see it in her expressive eyes that shine all too often with tears. The never-ending tension in my neck has me rubbing away the pain. It matches the pain in my chest. I want to fix us. I just don't know fucking how.

Like a creepy-ass peeping Tom, I climb out of my Tahoe and stalk over to the windows. She's smiling. Always so pretty when she smiles. Her round ass shakes as she dances to the music that plays through the kitchen speakers. Justin Timberlake or some shit. I don't care what it is…it makes her happy. She's never happy anymore. I stare at her ass as she wiggles it, standing at the kitchen island and flipping through a recipe book.

My cock is hard, but it's my heart that seems to thrum back to life. She's so playful in this moment. If I could shed some of this bitterness, I would go in there, sneak up behind her, and hug her from behind. I'd rub against her and whisper dirty shit in her ear. I would strip her down and fuck her over the island. Like old times. For a moment, hope burns inside of me. Would she accept me?

Of course she would.

She's my wife.

With newfound determination, I stalk around to the back door. I walk inside and dump my messenger bag on the bench by the door. Then, I stride into the kitchen on a mission. After four months of no sex, I'm going to fuck my wife. I'm not sleeping on the couch for the third week in a row. I'm going to fix this.

The moment her attention snaps to mine, her curls bobbing at the action, her smile falls. The glimmering in her green eyes dulls. Those sultry, pouty lips press into a firm, disappointed line.

"You were out late," she says softly.

An accusation.

The tension grabs hold of me again and I'm suddenly feeling defensive. "I had to work."

"Of course. And did you lose your tie along the way?" Her green eyes flare with hurt.

I'm a mess. My tie is gone. I've been running my fingers fitfully through my hair. I'm sure it looks worse than it is. I may have eyeballed my student and had a few hot fantasies, but I'd never act on them. Never.

"Vale…" My voice is husky, a twinge of guilt. "Baby."

Chapter
FOUR

Vale

Vaughn's not a cheater. And neither am I. But how do I explain the burning I'd felt not but a couple of hours before being with Aiden? How the hell does he explain the just-fucked hair and missing clothes? An ache, deep inside my chest crushes me.

We're breaking.

Little by little at first, but now it's happening all too quickly. Too many little holes in our boat. We're sinking. It'll be over in a flash. I'm devastated. I'm also slightly relieved. I am so tired of this. The fights. The silent brooding. The showers where I sob all alone. I can't take it anymore.

"Vale," he says again, his voice raspy. A plea almost. I want to go to him, but his hands are fisted in anger. He doesn't want me. Those gentle hands that had wrought out so much pleasure over the past eight years now are foreign to me.

"I think you should go," I whisper, my tears welling up, blurring his handsome form.

He walks my way, tension rolling off him in waves. When he's close enough to touch, I look down at our feet. His dress shoes are on either side of my boots. At one time, I would've thought it cute and grabbed my phone to snap a picture. Now, I'm staring at two strangers' feet. We're not picture worthy.

"I don't want to go." His words are cracked and sad. A glimmer of hope bleeds inside of me.

His palm finds my hip and I flinch. It's been months since we touched. I don't even remember the last time we kissed. Emotion clogs my throat as his thumb caresses my hip. When I chance a look up at him, his intense brown eyes bore into me. Rugged yet refined, my husband is a looker. He carries a powerful aura that makes you want to be in his protective embrace. An embrace I've been denied for far too long. My mind drifts to earlier in the shop when Aiden had held me. He was warm and comforting. I'd needed that more than air in that moment.

I'm the cheater.

I wanted Aiden to kiss me.

"We're broken," I whisper.

His other hand finds the side of my neck and he cradles me as though I'm precious. A choked sob rattles from me. "We're not broken," he assures me despite the way his voice trembles. "We're just cracked. All we need is a little glue. We'll be good as new."

I want to believe him.

"We just need time," he says, his hot breath against my cheek. "We're fixable, baby."

His lips find mine and he kisses me softly. The apology in his kiss has me moaning in relief. For so long I've craved his touch and now that he's giving it to me, it doesn't feel real. His tongue sweeps across mine and I moan again. The sound seems to encourage him because his palms find my ass and he lifts me. Our kiss grows frantic as he carries me through the kitchen and past the living room where I'd already laid out his pillow and blanket. He totes me upstairs to the bedroom he hasn't slept in for weeks.

"Vaughn," I whisper against his mouth. "I've missed this."

He growls in agreement as he sets me to my feet beside the bed. We tear at each other's clothes until we're naked. Then, he's mauling me like he's desperate for me. I know the feeling and I claw at his shoulders, needing him inside me more than anything else in this world.

"I need you," I moan.

"I'm going to taste you first," he rumbles.

"No," I beg. "Just…"

His cock rubs between my pussy lips. I'm wet and eager. I don't want foreplay. I just want him.

"Baby," he says, his voice pained. I hear the plea in his voice and I ignore it. Old habits are hard to break.

I dig my heels into his hard ass and urge him inside me. We both groan in pleasure. His thickness stretches me and I feel like he's taking my virginity all over again. He slides deep inside me where he belongs.

"I wanted to lick your pretty pussy," he complains.

Curls of defensiveness swirl inside me, raising my hackles. "Just make love to me." Just put a baby inside me. As soon as the thought enters my mind, guilt surges through me. He reads my mind because he tenses. I swear his cock softens, but then he bites on my bottom lip and fucks me hard.

Tears of disappointment leak from my eyes. It's not just him. It's me. I'd grown so fixated on having a baby, I made sex a mission. It wasn't fun. It was a means to an end. And even now, knowing he's physically unable to give me a baby, I hold out hope anyway. I've given him a mission he will fail. A failure I'll ultimately resent him for.

He was wrong.

He can't fix us.

We're stuck in a constant loop.

His breath becomes ragged and he grunts out his release. I make small moans, even making one louder at the end. Pretending. I'm pretending with my husband. This isn't love. This isn't fair. This is another head game he's accused me of playing. It doesn't feel like a game. It feels like my life and I'm failing at it.

He stills after his cock empties and then his eyes are on mine. "I'm sorry I can't give you what you want." The bitterness in his tone has me biting on my bottom lip to keep a sob from escaping.

"It's fine," I whisper. It is. I've made peace with it. Or so I thought.

His expression becomes stony and he pulls out. I watch as he pads into the bathroom and turns on the shower. I should join him. I should apologize. I should fix us.

Instead, I roll over and cry into my pillow.

I'm busy this morning in the coffee shop. My new muffins are a hit too. Turns out, Aiden was right. Taking off my curtains that I slaved over to sew was a step in the right direction. Several new customers didn't realize I was open for business. But with the curtains gone and the window open, their curiosity got the better of them. When I finally get a break, I check my phone for any missed calls.

Nothing from Vaughn.

My eyes burn with threatening tears. He slept on the couch last night and was gone this morning. I haven't spoken to him since we had sex. Guilt is eating me alive. I want to message him and apologize, but I don't know what to say. That I'm sorry for wishing we could have a baby? That my obsession to get pregnant has ruined us and it's all my fault?

I open my messages but instead of texting my husband, I text Aiden.

Me: You were right.

His response is immediate, making me smile.

Aiden: I'm always right.

Smug ass.

Me: The beautiful curtains were hiding my goods.

Aiden: The hideous curtains were hiding the

beautiful goods.

My cheeks flood with heat. I'm flirting with my employee. It's awful, but it's the best I've felt in months.

Me: I made lemon berry muffins. Sold out by nine.

Aiden: Did you save me one, boss?

Me: I saved you two.

Aiden: Good girl.

Stop, Vale.

Just stop.

Me: I have to go. Customer is coming in.

It's a lie, but I need to stop.

Aiden: I'm fucking happy to hear it. Don't worry, Vale, we'll revive your dying shop.

Me: Thank you.

I'm just worried he's going to revive my dying heart in the process. And where will that leave my marriage?

Chapter
FIVE

Aiden

Vaughn is especially broody today. When he caught me texting, he glowered at me until I tucked my phone away in my pocket. Probably for the better. Gave me an opportunity to admire his tight ass as he wrote notes on the board. Judging by the way several girls in class sit with their tits out and attention on our professor, I'm not the only one checking out his hot ass. Now that he's forced me to sit up front, I get a stellar view of his perfect body. My eyes roam up to the back of his head. Today, he's tense and put together. Not a hair out of place or a wrinkle in his shirt. Compared to last night where he seemed to be fraying, today he appears cool and untouchable.

I'm still looking at his ass when I realize everyone

is leaving. I haven't paid an ounce of attention to anything he's talked about. I'm so fucked in this class.

"Mr. Blakely." Vaughn pins me with an angry glare. "Stay put."

I let out an annoyed huff. "Yep." Great, another lecture.

A couple of girls giggle at me as they leave and I smirk at them. When they're gone, Vaughn's penetrating stare is on mine. He strides over to me with purpose. Intent burning in his brown-eyed stare. His white dress shirt hugs his toned body perfectly. I lick my lips because he's fucking hot and he does my head in.

"Anyone ever tell you your head's in the clouds, Blakely?" He stands all too close to my desk. I'm practically eye level with his dick. I don't miss the bulge in his slacks. Biting the inside corner of my lip, slightly amused, I lift my eyes to meet his. I arch a challenging brow that says, *Your dick's flying high too, Professor.*

He sits on the edge of my desk, his scent enveloping me. A cologne I recognize but can't put my thumb on permeates the air. I lick my lips because he smells too good. His eyes narrow, burning with unmasked desire, as he watches me.

"You have a smart mouth," he growls.

I laugh. "I didn't say anything."

He cracks his neck and looks hot as fuck doing it too. "You didn't have to. Your eyes say what you want to say. Your lips twitch. I know what you want to say and it's smartass shit."

"Smartass shit my dad should whip my ass for?" I challenge playfully.

The corners of his lips turn up like he wants to grin. It makes me want to see what this man looks like when he smiles. "You don't pay attention. You're going to fail my class. Do you even know what I talked about?"

"Economics?"

This earns me a smirk. "Smartass." He stands from the desk and motions for me to follow him. "Come on. We're getting out of here."

"Why?" I challenge as I rise, my eyes on his ass.

"I'm going to tutor you and I don't want to do it here."

I grab my bag and hoist it over my shoulder. "I could eat."

"And I could use a beer."

Chuckling, I follow him out of the classroom. "It's barely noon, man."

"When you have to deal with brats like Aiden Blakely, you need a drink after," he retorts, a wicked glint in his eyes.

Is Professor Jerkoff flirting with me?

I smirk at him and push out of the building. The icy chill of the wind has me pulling up my hood and grumbling. Vaughn stalks over to his SUV and we both climb in. His vehicle smells like him and I like it. It should feel weird being in his car with him, but I like the way he relaxes in his seat as though the weight of the world is no longer on his shoulders. He pulls on some sunglasses and then backs out of the parking spot. I push back my hood and watch him from the corner of my eyes. That cord of muscle along the side of his neck just begs to be licked.

Buzzzz.

I pull out my phone to see a text from my brother.

Ugly Twin: Steph is getting antsy. Says get your ass over for dinner or else. She wants to show off her ring.

Smiling, I tap out a reply.

Me: Tell Steph I'm busy juggling school and my new job. I'll get by soon.

Ugly Twin: Everything okay?

Compared to a week ago, it is. I'm enjoying my

time with Vale at the coffee shop and finally have my professor relaxing a little. They're both hot as fuck, which doesn't help on my whole sexuality confusion, but I suppose it's a good problem to have.

Ugly Twin: Dad said you've met someone. He was telling me you were smitten with her. I wonder, though, if she's really a her. Is she a he?

A chuckle escapes me. Of course my twin knows me better than anyone. It's like we share a brain half the time.

Me: It's complicated.

Ugly Twin: Always has been with you. Spill, asshole. Don't make me beg like a chick for all the juicy gossip.

Me: I like my boss. She's cute as hell and her smiles are everything.

Ugly Twin: Wanting your boss IS complicated. Why do I feel like there's more to this story?

Me: I also want to fuck the shit out of my professor. He's probably as old as Dad too.

Ugly Twin: HA! I knew it. Dad is gonna shit. I'm not the only one giving him gray hairs around here.

I glance over at Vaughn. His jaw clenches as he drives. Always so serious, this man. And I joke about him being old, but if I had to guess, he's in his late thirties.

Me: I'm no closer to figuring out whether I prefer men or women.

Ugly Twin: It's okay not to choose, bro. It's okay if you like both. That's the whole meaning of bisexual. It's a thing. Aiden Blakely isn't the pioneer in liking both chicks and dicks at once.

I snigger and send him the middle finger emoji.

Me: Speaking of dicks, you're the biggest one I know, Anthony.

Ugly Twin: You mean I have the biggest dick you know of.

Me: We're twins, remember?

Ugly Twin: Mine's bigger.

Me and this idiot will go round and round about this until the day we die. I remember being thirteen and we measured. Our little dicks at the time were exactly the same size just like everything else about us. Anthony was pissed. Dad was even more pissed when he walked in on us measuring our dicks. Got us both with the belt that day.

Me: Gotta go. Give Steph some tongue for me.

This time, I'm the one who gets the middle finger emoji.

I'm grinning as we pull up to a tavern. I lift a brow at Vaughn. "I'm only eighteen."

He pulls off his sunglasses and laughs. Fuck if that laugh doesn't get my dick hard. "Yeah, thanks for the reminder, kid. And I know the owner. It's fine. You can drink water."

We climb out and the first thing I notice is the change in his gait. He's no longer stiff and angry. My professor is loosening up. I bring my bag inside because he claims we're here to study.

The inside of the tavern is dark. Walls, tables, floors. All of it is dark wood and each table is lit up by a hanging light that doesn't put out much light. It's cozy and warm, though, a nice contrast to the bitter wind outside. Vaughn saunters to the back away from everyone and settles into one of the high-backed booths. I sit down across from him and lift a brow in question.

"Studying, huh?" I pick up a drink menu. "I can barely read the words in here."

Vaughn smirks at me. "All you need to do is listen. Just like in class. You blanked out back there. I'm just going to lecture you here. One on one. You can't avoid me."

I shake my head, biting back a snort of laughter.

"You underestimate my daydreaming abilities."

"You really don't like econ, do you?"

"It's not that I don't like your class, I just don't like college in general. It's boring. I'd rather be doing something. Anything else." I shrug and turn my gaze back to the menu.

We're silent until a waiter shows up. He's old and reeks of cigarette smoke.

"Well, if it isn't my boy, Vaughn," the old man says, chuckling. "Haven't seen you in years."

"Been busy," Vaughn says. "How's Ethel, Jim?"

Jim frowns. "Cancer took her last year. She fought hard until the end."

"I'm sorry to hear that," Vaughn mutters. "I wish you had called me. I would've gone to the funeral."

Jim swats at the air, his big belly jiggling. "Nah, she didn't want that kind of attention. I kept it small like she would have wanted. How've you and the missus been?"

Vaughn stiffens and I swear his teeth are gritting to dust. "Seen better days."

"Last I saw, you two were trying for a baby. How'd that work out for ya?"

"It didn't," Vaughn says icily.

Jim stands there awkwardly. "I'm sorry."

"It's fine. I'll have whatever's your best on tap. Get the kid a water," he replies.

"I'll have what he's having," I grunt out to Jim, my voice deep and every bit as gravelly as Vaughn's.

Jim chuckles and walks off.

"I'm corrupting my student," Vaughn groans.

"Your student needs a beer to get through his economics tutoring."

"Economics isn't so bad. You just have to give it a chance," he says. "What is it you really want to do, anyway? You've mentioned that you hate college, but what is calling to you?"

I shift in my seat, shrugging. "Are you going to judge me like my dad?"

His eyes narrow. "I'm not your dad."

"I always wanted to own my own restaurant."

My words seem to personally offend him because his nostrils flare and he crosses his arms over his chest. "A restaurant is hard work. Requires a hefty startup. They fail more often than not."

Wow, broken record much?

Sounds like he and my dad have the same damn rule book that the rest of us aren't privy to.

"You asked," I snap.

He lets out a sigh. "Sorry. It's just...I've heard

this before and let's just say, it didn't work out for that person."

"Maybe that person didn't want it as bad as I do," I say coolly.

He leans forward and pins me with a fiery glare. "She wanted it. She wanted it so fucking bad. I told her no and she begged. I caved and now it's failing. As much as I've wanted to tell her I told you so, I've held back. But you? I can warn you. They fail more often than not. Word of advice," he barks out. "Go to college. Get your degree. Make money on something reliable."

I cross my arms and glower at him. "Like you? Because you're so goddamned happy."

Fury flashes in his eyes, but Jim decides to show up with our beers. He sets them down clumsily and they slosh out onto the tabletop.

"Food for you, fellas? We make fried pickles now," he says proudly.

"Bring us some of those," I tell him. "And whatever else you got. I'm starving."

Jim waddles off, leaving me alone with my brooding teacher.

"Are you always so…mercurial?" I ask as I pick up my beer.

He lifts his glass and chugs it rather than answering

me. I watch as his Adam's apple bobs in his throat. I'd like to lick that too. Too bad this guy is an icy motherfucker. I'd love nothing more than to get hot with him.

Truth is, though, I'm not sure I would know what to do with a man like him. I've been with guys around my age. Guys who are down for a quick fuck or blowjob. I haven't ever been with a man who radiates so much emotion. Something tells me you can't dip your toes in with a man like Vaughn Young. You'll drown. He's deep.

Not to mention, married.

I sip my beer and wonder what kind of woman marries a man like Vaughn. Is he a total dick to her? Is she one of those nagging types who makes him eye-fuck students because he can't get laid by his own wife?

We're quiet until Jim brings out some baskets of greasy shit. I'm hungry as hell, though, and can't be choosy. I order some shots of tequila, earning a death glare from Vaughn.

"We're supposed to be learning," he grunts.

"Lecture away, Professor."

He grits his teeth but then begins talking. At first, I'm fixated on his mouth. His lips and his tongue when he licks away a lingering crumb from his food. But then, I begin to notice his passion. I start to hear what it is he's so passionate about. He discusses economics in a way that isn't so fucking boring. Hearing his excitement has me interested. It kind of reminds me of how my stepmother, Ava, would help me in high school. She was always so good at breaking my math down so I understood it. Vaughn is the same way. I'm already piecing together how I'll correct my assignment I'd been struggling with because some of the dots are beginning to connect finally.

We move from economics to business. He tells me about the different things that go into owning your own business. When he discusses marketing, I finally feel as though I can hold my own in the conversation. We discuss my father's advertising firm. Turns out, he knows of my father. Jim brings us drink after drink.

"Fuck, it's hot in here," I groan as I grab the bottom of my hoodie and pull it over my head. As soon as it's off and I toss it onto the seat beside me, I feel Vaughn's heated stare on me. Our eyes meet and fire burns inside me.

I'm going to fuck this man.

Or, he's going to fuck me.

Someone is getting fucked.

Chapter
SIX

Vaughn

"I gotta take a piss," Aiden says, his voice gravelly and almost lazy sounding.

I give him a clipped nod but don't even have the ability to hide my blatant desire for him. He'd lost the hoodie and that was a big fucking mistake. His black T-shirt hugs his muscular chest and my dick's been at attention ever since. When he slides out of the booth and stands, I rove my gaze over his muscular frame.

"Want me to take a picture so you have something to look at while I'm gone?" he teases, heat flaming in his steel-colored blue eyes.

"Smug ass," I grunt in response.

He laughs and saunters away. My phone buzzes and I pick it up.

Vale: I've been doing some thinking. I think I'll go stay with my sister.

My heart clenches in my chest. Are we really at this point? I mean, I'm in a bar lusting over my student when I should be fixing my marriage. But I don't know how. I tried last night and we fell right back into the same pattern. She was crying after my shower last night and I couldn't face her.

I'm unable to give her children.

That's the big fucking wedge that has divided us.

Her resentment toward me is ever-present and my disappointment in myself makes my attitude suck. We're no longer good together.

Me: I'd rather you not.

Really, Vaughn? I'd rather you not? That's a shitty attempt to fight for your wife if I ever saw one.

Me: Baby, please. Don't go to Tina's. Just stay at home. We'll talk tonight.

Vale: Our talking is no longer working. Nothing is working.

Me: I love you, though, Vale. We're in a bad place, but we can get out of it.

Starting with not having a fucking date with my student.

Vale: I love you too, but it doesn't change the fact

we've drifted too far apart. A customer just came in. We can discuss this later.

I don't respond and soon Aiden is back. His eyes are glassy from the alcohol. Kid isn't even old enough to drink. What the fuck am I even doing?

"Who killed your cat? You look like you're going to cry," he jokes.

I grit my teeth and slam back the rest of my beer. "We're done here. I need to sober up and get home."

"We're done?" he asks, hurt flashing in his expressive eyes.

Yes, I'm done with all this. A weak moment. I can't go down this road, not if I'm trying to fix my marriage. I'm an asshole.

"Done." I slap some cash down on the table. "When Jim comes back, pay the tab and I'll run you back to campus."

His eyes harden as I slide out of the booth and storm over to the bathroom. I stumble slightly and curse at myself for drinking too much. Once inside the bathroom, I piss and then wash my hands. I stare at my reflection and am haunted by the man staring back at me. I don't know him. He's unhappy as fuck. Someone killed the real Vaughn along the way.

Infertility.

I grit my teeth and turn on the cold water. Splashing my face, I try to sober up that way. It doesn't work and I hang my head in shame. I shouldn't be here with Aiden. I'm so fucked in the head.

The door opens and I turn to face off with the man who has my stomach in knots. He storms over to me, grabbing my shirt, and fists it before pushing me against the wall. His eyes flare with heat as his body presses against mine. Hard. Everywhere.

"We're not over, Professor. We're just beginning," he growls.

I open my mouth to protest, but then his hot-as-fuck lips are on mine. Demanding and controlling. He kisses me, stealing a groan from me, and then his tongue is on mine. I'm stunned by his sudden kiss. Horrified even that I'm kissing someone other than Vale. I grip his T-shirt, infuriated at his forcing my hand like this. When I go to push him away, I learn he's stronger than me. Stubborn bastard. His hips rub against mine and I moan, sounding like a needy prick. It feels too good to push him away. He tastes too good too. At some point, he manages to overpower me and our hips work in tandem to rub against each other. His dick is hard and aching as it rubs against mine, which is just as fucking eager. My hands are desperate and I grip his ass, urging him closer.

He bites my lip, hard and unrelenting. A growl escapes me as I tear from his kiss. His mouth, the greedy fuck, attacks my neck. He sucks my flesh between his teeth and I swear to hell I almost come. It feels that good.

And then it hits me.

If this fucker leaves a hickey on me, Vale will go fucking nuts. Everything she ever worried about will have come true. I push against his chest and shove him away.

"Stay the hell away from me," I snarl, rage quickly replacing the lust burning through me.

He glowers at me. "You want this. Your marriage is over. You don't have to say it, anybody can see that. There's something between us and I'll be damned if I ignore it."

"Fuck you," I snap. "You know nothing about me."

He stalks forward. "I know your dick is hard for me."

Anger explodes within me and I swing at him. My knuckles clip his cheekbone just below his eye and he stumbles back. Hurt flashes in his eyes. I feel like a fucking monster.

"Aiden," I mutter, my fury quickly squelched.

He rubs at his face where I hit him and shakes his head. "No, man, I get it. Stay the fuck away. Duly noted." When he starts for the door, I grip his shoulder.

"I'll take you back to campus," I grit out.

He looks at his watch. "I'm already late for work. I'll walk."

"You can't go to work drunk," I argue. "You'll get fired."

He sneers at me. "And you can't make out with students either. You'll get fired. Looks like we're both shitty humans with no respect for the law. But don't worry, your job is no longer in jeopardy. I'm out."

As he leaves, I can't help but feel as though I've fucked over yet one more person in my life who doesn't deserve it.

Goddammit.

Chapter
SEVEN

Vale

When the store empties out, I check my phone again and stare at Vaughn's texts. Sometimes, when we talk through text, I feel like we say more than when we're face to face. He wants me to stay. Yet, when we're together, we barely speak to one another. Us having sex last night for the first time in four months felt like progress, but we slipped right back into the same old routines. It's not just his fault. It's mine too. As soon as we were naked, I was right back to all those months where we desperately tried to have children. I religiously stalked an infertility forum where those women were hard-core. I became hard-core too. They were my friends and talked me through every aspect of trying to have a baby.

I relied on them instead of him.

He was just a means to get what I wanted.

A baby.

Bitterness sours my belly. At first, he was so good and supportive over it all. He wanted a baby every bit as much as I did. Vaughn read the books. Took vitamins I forced down his throat. Had sex with me every time I said we had to. It was fun at first, stripping down and racing to the finish. I enjoyed how he'd sit with me, my ass on a pillow holding his sperm inside me, and plan all the names of our future children.

But it soon got old.

He grew agitated.

I was desperate.

What started out as fun became a point of contention between us. We'd fight about my desperation and his cool aloofness. Drift, drift, drift. It got to the point where he'd have sex with me, empty his seed, and then leave to go grade papers. We barely spoke. And then, after a meltdown when he suggested adoption, we stopped having sex altogether.

Until last night.

Last night was an opportunity to fix us. To start over. And I just became desperate once more. Prayed to God that this time, we'd stick. That we'd get pregnant and it would save our marriage because we'd be happy.

I twist my wedding ring around my finger and let out a sigh. We'll never be happy again, I'm afraid. It's too far gone. A year ago, I never looked at another man. Now, I get flustered and breathless whenever I'm in the same room with Aiden Blakely. I never saw myself as one to step out on my marriage, but most days, I feel like I'm the only one there playing house. Vaughn long ago left me. Mentally checked out of our marriage.

As if my thoughts summon him, the bell chimes at the front door. I peek my head out the door of the back kitchen to see Aiden storming into the shop. His dark brows are furled together in an angry way I've never seen and his hair is tousled as if he's been running his fingers through it. It's cold outside and yet he's not wearing his hoodie. He has it looped around the strap of his messenger bag that's across his chest.

"You're late," I observe as he stalks past me.

Odd. He's always so friendly.

He tosses his stuff into my office chair and then crosses his arms over his chest. His cheeks and nose are red from the cold and his steely eyes blaze with emotion. Being under his heated gaze, I feel my heart rate speed up. I nervously bite on my bottom lip and lift a brow as if to ask him what's wrong. But my throat is clogged and I don't know that I can speak.

"Are you okay?" I manage to choke out.

His eyes narrow and he prowls my way, his hands falling to his sides as he approaches. Whatever is going on with him has caused him to make a decision. And that decision feels like it might be me. My skin heats at that thought and then guilt surges through me.

I'm not ready!

He stops just as our chests nearly touch. With my heavy breathing, my breasts brush against the hardness of him. I tilt my head up to look at him despite what a bad idea that is. His gaze softens as he regards me. Then he lifts a hand to tuck away a strand of my hair behind my ear.

"You're so beautiful," he murmurs, his voice husky and raw.

When was the last time I've heard that? Certainly not from Vaughn. Guilt splashes cold water on my heart and I look down, anything to get away from his eyes. His palm slides into my hair and he grips it against my skull. I let out a sharp gasp when he tilts my head back, his fiery gaze burning into me.

"I'm going to kiss you," he tells me, his smug tone making my stomach flop.

"You can't," I breathe. "I'm married."

He smirks. "No one said you had to kiss back."

His full lips press to mine and I let out a surprised sound. He seems to take this as an invitation and sweeps his tongue across my lips. Heat burns through me from my lips all the way to my core and I grip the front of his T-shirt that molds to his sculpted physique.

"You taste like alcohol," I murmur against his mouth.

"You taste like snickerdoodles," he growls back.

I let out a small giggle because I'd eaten one before he came in. He nips at my bottom lip, silencing me. Then, he tugs on it with his teeth before trailing kisses along my jaw to my ear. When his teeth tug at my lobe, I let out a groan of pleasure.

Crap.

This is happening.

I should push him away. Make it stop.

He sucks on my flesh and I whimper. His palm goes to my ass and grips me, pulling at my cheek. It makes me feel exposed and realize how wet I've gotten from this heated kiss. We definitely have to stop.

Vaughn and I may be headed for divorce, but we're not there yet.

The bell chimes, indicating a customer, and I tense. "Aiden, I need to get out there."

He sucks on my neck hard, making me cry out. "They can wait."

"No, I—" I start but then hear someone curse.

"What the fuck?" a familiar voice roars. "What in the actual fuck?"

Aiden is ripped from me and is thrown against the island I used to roll out dough. A pan goes careening to the floor with a loud, deafening clatter. I stare horrified as my husband charges for Aiden again.

"No!" I cry out. "Vaughn, stop!"

He grabs ahold of Aiden's throat and shoves him against a wall. Aiden throws a punch in Vaughn's side, causing him to howl. They're going to beat each other up and it's all my fault.

"Vaughn," I plead as I grab hold of the back of his shirt. "I'm sorry. I had a moment of weakness. We can talk this out."

The muscles in his neck twitch with fury and then he turns his murderous gaze on me. I can smell the liquor on his breath, which confuses me. He should be at work. Not drunk and in my shop.

"How do you two know each other?" he seethes.

"He's my employee. The one I told you about."

His green eyes soften. "You never told me his name."

Aiden grunts, but Vaughn doesn't release him.

"I did," I whisper. "You weren't listening."

"Did you tell her I'm your student?" Aiden hisses, hurt lacing his voice. "Did you tell her we got shitfaced and made out in a bar bathroom?"

Vaughn winces as the horror of his words sinks in.

"What?" I choke out. "I don't understand."

Vaughn releases Aiden and steps back, stumbling slightly as he runs his fingers through his hair. A purple mark is forming on his neck and I absently touch the spot Aiden was just kissing.

Aiden grits his teeth and straightens his shirt. "It appears I've been crushing on a fucking married couple."

"You're gay?" I ask at the same time Vaughn asks, "You're straight?"

My husband and I share a shameful look.

"I'm bi," Aiden snaps. "It's a thing." He rubs at the back of his neck, shaking his head.

"Did you give him that?" I demand, my words

shaking as I point at the hickey that's forming on Vaughn's neck. I knew back in college he'd been with guys and dated a few here and there before us. It never occurred to me he'd cheat on me with a man, though. In my head, all those late nights at the office were with some bimbo blond student.

Not this.

Not Aiden.

"We kissed and it got heated," Aiden grunts. "Then, he got mad and I left."

Vaughn shoots him a murderous glare. "And then you came to make out with my wife to get back at me."

"I didn't know she was your wife," Aiden bites back. He implores me with his eyes. "I didn't know."

Vaughn's stare grows soft and he looks so lost. Exactly how I feel. Aiden appears to be hurt as well. We just really made a mess of things. My husband and I cheated on each other with the same man. This is some Maury Povich stuff right here.

"I should go," Aiden mutters, his brows furling together.

Vaughn grips his bicep, almost as if he can't bear him to leave. Their eyes meet and heat blazes between them. Seeing that look on my husband's face after so long makes my heart squeeze. Then, I realize it's no longer for me.

"Don't go," I murmur, drawing both their attention.

Both men stare intently at me, as if I have the answers to this mess. I don't, but I know sending Aiden away isn't going to fix anything. If anything, we need to talk about this.

"You're both clearly drunk. We'll close the shop early, take some coffee with us so you can sober up, and talk about this at the house over dinner. The three of us." I bite on my lip. Both men watch the action with similar expressions. Want. It urges me forward. "We're clearly in this together and the only way to sort through it is together. If Vaughn and I were both kissing you, there's something clearly broken about our marriage."

"Me," Aiden says bitterly. "I'm the one breaking it."

Vaughn turns and regards him, his thumb gently brushing over Aiden's bicep. "We were already broken. You didn't break anything." Vaughn turns to me. "Right?"

I nod and swallow. "Right."

The tension leaves Aiden's shoulders. "Okay then. We'll talk. But I want some of those snickerdoodle cookies and the lemon berry muffin you promised me."

Vaughn releases him and glances around the

kitchen. "You're selling food? I thought it was just a coffee shop."

Aiden snorts. "Keep up, man. I made her tear down those ugly-ass curtains too. We're sprucing up the place and making it better."

My husband's brows lift in surprise. "But you made those curtains."

"They were lovely," I say with a pout.

"The customers didn't think so," Aiden argues. "Admit it."

"They visit more without them," I say with a grumble.

Vaughn winks at me. He once gently tried to tell me the curtains were a little much for a coffee shop and I cried. I fight a smile. At first, he looks like he might approach me, but then he fists his hands and holds back. I'm tired of him holding back.

The heat in the kitchen burning from these two men has me escaping. Coffee. They both need coffee or in their inebriated state we may all do something we can't undo.

And why does that thought send a flutter of butterflies dancing in my belly?

Chapter
EIGHT

Aiden

My brother keeps texting me, his jokes a thin veil for his worry. We have the whole twin shared brain thing going on because it's like he knew the moment things blew up with Vaughn and me. I've ignored him, but now that I'm sitting in the backseat of Vaughn's SUV as Vale drives us to their house, I'd like to escape the awkward tension.

> *Me: I'm alive. Call off the search.*
> *Ugly Twin: Asshole. What's up?*

An ache forms in my chest as I reply.

> *Me: Remember my complicated confusion?*
> *Ugly Twin: You have the hots for your boss and for your professor. I remember.*
> *Me: I kissed them both.*

Ugly Twin: Sounds hot. Keep it casual so it doesn't get any more complicated.

Me: Turns out they're married.

He sends me some wow emojis.

Ugly Twin: Dude. Walk away. You'll have double the trouble if their spouses find out.

Me: Anthony, they're married to each other.

The dots move and then stop. Move and then stop. I lift my eyes to catch Vale watching me in the mirror. She turns her attention back to the road but not before her cheeks turn pink.

Ugly Twin: Aiden. Just...no.

Irritation flits through me. Easy for him to say. He's with the woman he loves. Went through hell to get her too. It was messy and not socially accepted at first. I was there for him every step of the way.

Me: I can smell your judgment from here. Stinks, bro.

Ugly Twin: I just don't want you to get hurt. If a married couple was cheating on each other to be with you, that's fucked up. Too much baggage. You deserve better than that.

I grit my teeth and nearly crush my phone in my fist.

Me: I'm not your little brother you have to look

out for. We're the same fucking age. I can make my own decisions just like you made yours.

Ugly Twin: Calm down, man. I'm just fucking worried, okay?

Me: Well, stop your fucking worrying. I'll figure it out.

Ugly Twin: Dad is going to throw a shit fit if he finds out.

Me: It's none of Dad's business who I fuck.

We roll to a stop in front of a cute bungalow house. The yard is kept nicely with lots of colorful flowers and trimmed shrubs. It represents the ideal happy marriage. Messy Aiden Blakely who couldn't cut it as a lawn boy is about to kick dirt all over their world.

Ugly Twin: Call me if you need to talk.

Me: Yep.

Vale lets out a ragged sigh before climbing out of the vehicle. Her cute ass jiggles in her tight leggings as she walks away. Vaughn falls into step beside me, neither of us speaking. We walk inside and she turns to face us.

"I'm going to go shower off the day and then we can talk." She wrings her hands in a nervous way.

I give her a nod and follow Vaughn into the

kitchen. When he pulls open a drawer with a bunch of takeout menus, I laugh.

"Hungry already?" I ask.

His jaw clenches and he regards me with a hot stare that has my dick lurching in my pants. Fuck these people with their needy stares and perfect mouths.

He clears his throat. "Yep, and pizza sounds better than that shitty bar food we ate."

Pizza sounds boring. I walk over to the fridge and start rummaging around. He closes the drawer when I pull out some chicken and vegetables.

"I'll cook us something." I gesture for the bar.

His brows rise. "I didn't know you cooked."

"You don't know a lot about me," I mutter as I wash my hands.

"I want to."

Our eyes meet and my lips quirk up on one side. "I guess that's why I'm here."

As I wash the chicken and find a cutting board, I can't help but notice the blankets and pillows on the couch. I don't say anything, but he follows my stare. His nostrils flare with embarrassment and he hurries to put the blankets away. I watch his ass in his slacks every time he bends over. Vale's kitchen is set up similar to how she keeps the coffee shop. I find what I need easily and soon the house smells of oriental stir fry.

Now that the coffee has sobered me up some, the reality of my situation is hitting me. I'm in this married couple's house to talk. Talk about what? The fact they both are attracted to me and kissed me. The fact that when I talked to them before I knew they were married, they made their spouse sound dreadful. These two people have guarded themselves so deeply against each other. It's fucking sad.

By the time the rice finishes up, Vale comes into the kitchen fresh-faced, with her hair still dripping. She wears black yoga pants and a white Nike tank top. Underneath, she wears a sports bra, but I can see her nipples, pert and erect, from a mile away. I flash her a grin and her cheeks blaze pink. When I glance over at Vaughn, he's watching our exchange with interest. Not jealousy. Maybe something akin to awe.

I wink at him and he smiles.

Fuck, is that man ever hot as hell when he smiles.

"I worked with what you had in the fridge. This is my stepmom's favorite. I make it a lot at home for her and my dad. My younger siblings hate it, though, and cry when they have to eat their veggies." I chuckle as I think about the twins and their adorable pouty faces.

"So you have siblings?" Vaughn asks as he sets to

opening a bottle of wine.

"Yeah, the twins, Jayden and Joseph are little terrors. The youngest is June. She's cute and spoiled but a happy baby." I smile fondly. June looks just like my stepmother, Ava. Dark brown hair. Big, innocent eyes. She has Dad wrapped around her little baby finger.

"You have another brother, though," Vale says. "The ugly twin."

I snort. "Yeah, Anthony."

"Two sets of twins?" Vaughn asks in astonishment.

"They run in the family," I tell him, grinning.

Surprisingly, dinner goes well. They each ask me lots of questions. Now that Vale knows I'm in college and a student under her husband, she asks more about my major and future plans. Vaughn seems keen on learning about my job and all I've done for the coffee shop for Vale. It's so obvious they're sneaking glimpses at the other through me.

"He's not old enough to drink," Vale remarks, humor dancing in her eyes as Vaughn pours me another glass of wine.

"Yeah, so I told him. He does what he wants," he grunts.

I shrug at her like, *See, he gets me.*

The room grows quiet and I finally let out a huff.

"Are we going to talk about the big elephant in the room?"

Vale stiffens and Vaughn drains his glass.

"What am I doing here?" This question goes unanswered too.

I give them each a pointed look.

"We're having dinner," Vale says weakly.

"We're getting to know you," Vaughn adds.

"You both are such bad liars," I say, chuckling. "Fine. We'll play this game. But we're going to play it from the living room and I'm going to need a stiffer drink than wine."

After the kitchen gets cleaned up and Vaughn changes out of his dress clothes into some sweats and a T-shirt, we congregate in the living room. I can't help but check out Vaughn. He looks nothing like the stuffy professor who's always on my ass. Fuck, he's hot, even if he does seem a little nervous. The cool, aloof professor does seem to get rattled and my being here does it to him.

I smirk at him. "Shall we?" I motion for the sofa. Vaughn makes a beeline for the recliner. Before he gets too far, I grab hold of the back of his T-shirt and pull him back. "Nope. Sofa."

He looks over his shoulder at me in confusion. I let him go and plop down right in the middle. They both eye me warily until I grin and pat the cushions on either side of me.

"If we're going to talk, I want you both close," I tell them boldly. "I want this 'discussion' to feel equal and not two against one."

They both nod and settle beside me. Vaughn unscrews the lid off his liquor bottle and takes a swig. He winces as the burn tears down his throat.

"Fuck, this is awkward," he complains.

I laugh and pat his thigh over his sweats. "It is." When I don't remove my palm from his thigh, he doesn't push it away. The helpless way he looks over at Vale would be comical if not for her wearing the same expression. "Should I go?" I ask, my voice husky.

Vale reaches over and clutches my hand. Her green eyes are wide as she bites on her bottom lip and shakes her head. "Stay. We want you to stay."

I turn and lift a brow at Vaughn.

He knocks back another swig of liquor and then licks his full lips. "Stay, Aiden."

Chapter

NINE

Vaughn

I don't know what the hell we're doing, but we're doing it. We have this hot-as-fuck guy sitting between us. Touching us. Making us laugh. He cooked us dinner, for crying out loud. Vale and I are in unchartered territory and Aiden is steering the ship. I don't want to fuck this up. With her. With him. Any of it. So I grit my teeth and keep my mouth shut.

"I'm not going to lie," Aiden rumbles, tilting his head back and staring up at the ceiling. "I have issues." He swallows and the hard knot of his Adam's apple bobs in his throat. I wet my lips because the urge to lick him is intense. My dick is aching in my sweats and I settle the bottle against it to hide my arousal.

When I glance over at Vale, she's blushing as she watches him with rapt attention. I don't know how we got ourselves in this fucked up situation, but we're here. This afternoon, she was as good as moving out and threatening divorce. Now? Now, we're here. Together. Exploring something new. And we're not fighting.

I flash her an encouraging smile that she returns. It makes my chest squeeze.

"I like women and I like men," he explains, his brows furling together. "I can't decide which I like better. I don't want to decide. Sometimes, I catch myself in situations where I have both. It isn't something I am able to navigate well because I'm still figuring it out myself." He squeezes my thigh and turns to look at me. His blue-gray eyes are liquid lust and my cock aches at his perfect face. "But I like you," he tells me. "The moment I saw you standing at the front of the classroom, I wanted to fuck you."

I let out a groan because my erection strains against my sweatpants for all to see. A fifth of Jack isn't going to hide my monster cock. His eyes flicker down to the bottle and he flashes me a wicked smile that does nothing to help the state of my erection.

"I'd like some of that," he says, his voice husky and filled with insinuation as he reaches for the bottle. His fingers are hot against mine as he grabs it. I let out a hiss when his knuckles brush against my dick.

My eyes catch Vale's and hers are swimming with lust. She watches us as if she has a prime seat at a porno. Her cheeks burn red when she catches me staring. God, she's so beautiful. I'd known it the first time I'd seen her smile. Something about her imperfect smile stole my heart in an instant.

"I love you," I mouth to her.

Her lashes flutter as she looks away, a smile tugging at her lips.

"And you," Aiden says, turning his attention to Vale. "The moment I saw you, I was completely smitten. So beautiful. Curvy and all smiles. Those leggings…" My cock twitches because the girl can rock a pair of leggings. "I wanted it all."

He takes a swig of the liquor and hands it to Vale. Her lips purse together in a pouty kiss as she sips the liquid fire. She chokes and both Aiden and I chuckle.

"Gah," she groans. "That's nasty."

She hands him the bottle and his fingers linger on hers as he takes it. This good-looking man in our living room seduces the both of us so easily. I'm in complete fucking awe.

"I'm not going to fuck either of you," he says with a frustrated huff.

Both she and I tense up. Her furrowed brows match mine.

"Nobody said anything about fucking," I grunt. But what I really want to ask is, *Why not?*

"For us to..." he trails off as if considering his words, "try anything, I need you two to be on the same page. Right now, you're not even in the same book."

"We're figuring our shit out," I grunt, a little too defensively.

She presses her lips together. "I told him I was leaving."

I gape at her and she shrugs.

"I'm tired of lying to ourselves," she whispers.

"You wouldn't be leaving if you didn't resent me so much," I snap back harshly.

She flinches as if my words physically wound her. Aiden frowns at me in disappointment. Instantly, I feel like an idiot.

"I'm sorry," I say to them both.

"Why do you resent him?" Aiden asks her softly.

Her eyes become glassy with tears and her nose turns pink. "I don't resent him."

"I can't give her a baby," I say bitterly. "It's all she wants."

"It's not all I want," she hisses, the tears freely streaking down her cheeks.

Now, I'm ashamed that we have a spectator in our never-ending fight.

"What do you want then?" Aiden asks, mimicking my thoughts. They come out curious and not confrontational, unlike how they'd come if I were to say them.

She swipes away her tears. "I just want to be happy."

"With a baby," I correct.

Her glare is icy, but Aiden doesn't let it deter him.

"So you take the baby out of the equation. Start there. Simple." He says this as if it's the easiest thing ever.

"I don't understand," she mutters.

"Fuck your husband and use a condom, Vale. Simple."

Her eyes fly to mine and her lips are parted at his bold words. "Okay."

"You have sex without the pressure of making a baby that you both haven't been successful at doing," he says. "Do you really want your marriage to dissolve? What happens when you move on and find someone else? What if the same problem arises? Do you keep running?"

Fuck, how old is this kid?

Eighteen.

He's eighteen fucking years old and already wiser than a man twenty years his senior.

Vale, chastised by his words, shoots me an apologetic look. I set the bottle down and reach across him to take her hand.

"Would last night have played out differently had I used a condom?" I ask, my voice shaking with nerves. "Would you have let me go down on you?"

"I, uh," she stammers, trying to tug her hand out of mine.

Aiden grips her hips and pulls her into his lap, bringing her closer to me. His arms wrap around her middle in an easy, affectionate way. With his muscular arms, holding her so she doesn't get away, I feel a little empowered to speak my mind. She's not shutting down per her usual. Her eyes are frantic as she implores me to understand. But I don't understand. I don't understand her obsession with getting pregnant.

"I wanted to make you come on my tongue," I tell her huskily. "I wanted to fuck you all night like old times."

Tears streak down her cheeks and her palm slides to my jaw. "I'm sorry."

I grab hold of the back of her neck and pull her to me, but she pushes against my chest. I freeze up and glower at her, embarrassment at being rejected making my hackles rise.

Aiden shakes his head. "You two are so fucked up." He sweeps her hair to the side, exposing her neck, and whispers against her flesh. "Kiss your husband, sweetheart. He won't bite. Well, maybe a little, but I bet you'd enjoy it."

She sticks her tongue out at him, making him chuckle. I find myself relaxing. Then, she turns her glowing green eyes my way and wets her lips with her tongue. Her tits jut forward as she leans in to kiss me. So primly and so her this past year. This was not how she was kissing him when I caught them earlier. Reaching up, I grip her jaw and draw her to me. My lips crush to hers and I kiss her in a demanding, possessive way that has her melting. A small moan whines from her.

"Closer," Aiden murmurs as he lifts her and manhandles her into my lap so that she's straddling me. "That's it." His palm runs up her spine and then down. It settles on my knee and he squeezes it.

I kiss my wife.

Hard and unrelenting.

As Aiden watches.

I'm hard as fuck and hope has me sliding my palms to her ass and squeezing.

"Fuck," I groan. "I've missed this."

Her small moans are breathy as she grinds her pussy against my aching dick. Through my sweats, I can feel every soft curve of her. Our breathing gets heavier and she's actively trying to get off by rubbing against me. When I can't take it anymore, Aiden grabs my hand and pushes a condom into it.

"Go fuck your wife. I'll sleep on the couch," he says.

I shoot him an apologetic look, but he shakes his head.

Picking Vale up, I storm through the house, eager to get her stripped of all her clothes. I kick the door shut and start peeling off her shirt before we even hit the bed. It's a mad, desperate scramble, but we're soon naked. Her eyes follow my hands as I tear the foil on the condom. Our gaze meets and I roll the rubber on my dick that's been hard as fuck all damn day. It twitches in my grip and she smiles.

"Lie back," I order, my voice raw with need. "I'm

going to eat that pussy you so selfishly denied me last night."

Her brow lifts as though she wants to challenge me, but then she gives in by letting her thighs part. I lick my lips as I appreciate the way her pussy glistens with her arousal. Leaning forward, I kiss her supple lips and then the middle of her chest. I trail soft kisses down to her belly button and nip at the flesh there. She gasps. I'm smirking when I look back up at her. I run my tongue down her lower stomach until I come to her smooth pussy. Kiss. Kiss. Kiss. I press small pecks to her clit over her pussy lips that has her spreading her trembling thighs even more as if to give me a peek at it hiding inside. I run my tongue up from her hole to her clit and she cries out, her back arching up in pleasure.

Feeling bolder, I start lapping at her essence I've missed so much. Her cunt always tastes so sweet. Like my little baker rubs some sugar between her thighs just for me. I realize I'm devouring her. Nipping and sucking. Licking and teasing.

"So beautiful," I whisper against her cunt before sucking her clit hard.

She thrashes against the covers as her orgasm hits violently. I haven't seen her lose control like this in at least a year. It's fucking breathtaking to watch.

Before she comes down from her high, I prowl up her body and tease her opening that's slick with her arousal with the tip of my dick. She hisses as I start pushing into her tight body.

"I hate condoms," she says, pouting. "I want to feel you."

I chuckle against her mouth and suck on her bottom lip. "Not today. Today you get fucked with a rubber."

She screams when I slam into her hard. Her nails rake over my flesh as I thrust into her. Our teeth clash together as we kiss in desperation. So close. We were so close to losing it all. All we needed was a fix. A little glue. Good as new.

I fuck her right into another orgasm and then I'm groaning out my own release. She's right. It does suck having to use the condom but at least she was here with me. We did this together.

With his help.

Aiden.

As if her thoughts mirror mine, she stares at me with her brows furrowing.

"Are we using him?" she whispers. "Is this wrong?"

"I don't know."

"Will you check on him?" she asks. "Make sure he's okay that…"

That I fucked her.

I want to roll my eyes at how stupid this sounds. My wife wants to make sure her would-be lover doesn't have his feelings hurt that she fucked her husband instead. And damned if I'm not pulling out of her and depositing the condom in the trash because I want to make sure he's okay too. He's every bit mine as he is hers. What we just did to him wasn't fair. I hope he understands.

"I'll be right back," I assure her as I tug on my sweats.

She nods and I slip out of our room. The lights have been turned off and I find Aiden stretched out on the couch.

"You okay?" I ask, my voice soft.

"I have to be." His words aren't bitter, just resigned.

"I'm sorry," I utter. "For this afternoon. For tonight. For everything."

"If it brought you two back together, it was worth it. Now go keep your wife warm before I do," he teases. His words are meant to joke, but I can hear his heart breaking from here.

Fuck.

"I'm sorry." I say it again, but this time I don't wait for a response. For the first time in months, I sleep in my own bed. With my wife. And we spend the whole night fucking like teenagers who don't want to get pregnant.

Chapter

TEN

Aiden

"Whats going on?" Stephanie whispers, leaning in from beside me on the pew.

I glance up at my brother's stunning fiancée. Silky blond hair. Bright blue eyes. Gorgeous as all hell. You'd never guess she's as old as my dad. Steph and her daughter Lacy could be sisters rather than mother and daughter.

"Nothing," I tell her, forcing a smile.

She frowns, not believing me for a second. "We'll talk after church."

I turn my attention back to Easton McAvoy. The most badass looking preacher I've ever seen. He's an ex-con slash biker turned man of God. And my brother's soon-to-be son-in-law. I bite back a snort of laughter. As if clued into my thoughts, Anthony shoots me a warning glare from the other side of Steph.

Easton goes on and on, but I'm not really listening. It's been a little over a week since I helped Vaughn and Vale get back together. She smiles more. He's less grumpy. Clearly they're making some progress. I've slowly backed away. I still check out her ass when she pulls baked goods out of the oven or linger my stare on her smile. And with Vaughn, I find myself inhaling his unique scent whenever he's near or trying to will my dick not to burst through my jeans any time his hard brown eyes are on mine. It's fucked up. I want them both, equally so, but they're married. I'd be a shitty human if I tried to get into the middle of that.

Which is why I took up Steph's ongoing offer to go with them to church. Maybe Easton can help guide me through this shit. When the service ends, I find Easton's questioning stare on me.

"Need to talk?" he mouths as he shakes someone's hand.

I give him a clipped nod and he makes a motion to his office. I try to make it past Stephanie, but she steals a hug from me. She smells good and I don't push away the affection.

"Whatever is going on will work itself out," she

tells me, squeezing me.

"Yeah, I know."

But I don't know. Am I always destined to be a third wheel? Always caught somewhere between this and that? Never deciding between being with a man or a woman? I can't figure out my life or make sense out of it. Sometimes I wish Dad were cool and would give me proper advice.

Pulling away from Steph, I ruffle Lacy's hair, earning a groan as I pass, and then shuffle past people in Easton's congregation. He and Lacy are the poster children for a good, wholesome God-fearing family. Aside from the rumor they were caught fucking in the church. Pastor McAvoy would never do something so devious. I'm sure it was all lies.

I escape the suffocating crowd and hide out in Easton's simple office. Pictures of his wife and son are everywhere and it makes me feel at home. My phone buzzes and I look to see a text from Vaughn.

Vaughn: Don't forget you have a test tomorrow. Did you even study?

I narrow my eyes at the text. I want to ask him if he wants to help me study but then determine I'd be an asshole tempting him into something he's trying desperately to avoid.

Me: Got it.

The dots move and then stop. Move and then stop.

Vaughn: Want any help?

I sit up and frown, typing out my reply.

Me: Everything okay with you and Vale?

Vaughn: We're fine.

I roll my eyes, imagining his icy, clipped response. I text her instead.

Me: Everything okay with you and Vaughn?

The dots move and then stop. Then I get a thumbs-up emoji.

Me: Vale…

Vale: We're fine.

Anxiety bubbles up inside me. They are not fine. Before I can respond to either, the office door opens and Easton strides in. He's dressed like a normal preacher with his black slacks and white button-down shirt. Aside from that, he's a total biker dude. Tattoos cover his forearms and backs of his hands. Some even peek up past his collar. He's a badass for sure.

"Aiden Blakely," he says, grinning as he shakes my hand. "Haven't seen you for dinner at Steph's in a while. College kicking your butt?"

"I have a tough professor." A grin tugs at my lips.

His brow arches and he smirks. "Guy or girl professor?"

My sexual proclivities have somehow been rumored down to Easton. These people are so fucking gossipy sometimes. "Male," I grunt. I watch his face for a reaction and find none. "Are you going to preach how it's a sin to lie with a man and that I'll get sent straight to hell?"

He rolls his eyes. "You've been watching too many movies, man."

"So if I told you I fuck dudes, you're not going to shun me from your church?"

"I'll smack you in the head if you keep cursing, but no, I'm not going to shun you." He shakes his head in disbelief. "I teach love."

I close my eyes and pinch the bridge of my nose, exhaling. "What if you love the wrong people?"

"I just told you, The Lord preaches love. Unconditional love at that. How are people supposed to love unconditionally if they are judging others for whom they love? They can't. So love is love and that's what God wants."

I can tell he's about to get on a tangent and make me highlight shit in a Bible, so I stop him with my hand held up. "Forgive me, Father, for I have sinned."

He snorts. "I'm a preacher, not a priest. We don't do confession here. What the hell is going on with you, man?"

Our eyes meet and concern flashes in his.

"My professor is married." I close my eyes. "To my boss. And I want them both." When I open my eyes again, he's frowning. So much for no judgment.

"You can't get involved in that, Aiden. That's coming from man to man."

"Because it's a sin," I huff out.

"Because it's wrong to get in the middle of someone's marriage."

"They're falling apart," I mutter weakly.

"And you think having an affair with you will hold them together?" As soon as he realizes that was exactly my hope, his expression softens. "What do you want me to say? That it's okay? You know I won't say that."

I grit my teeth. "I just want to know how to deal with this shit inside my head. In my heart. I want them, but I want them to be happy. They're trying, but…"

His brows crinkle together. "But?"

"But they're failing."

He sighs. "You could give them my number. I

counsel people sometimes. I'm not licensed, but I do it in a biblical sense. I'd be happy to guide them down the right path."

"The path that leads away from me," I say bitterly.

"If they're as fragile as you say they are, do you want to be the final wedge between them? Because that's what would happen. Jealousy would find its way inside the relationship. It might start out fun at first, but then three would become two. Someone would get hurt. Do you want to be the one responsible for that hurt, Aiden? What if you're the one who gets hurt in the end?" He scrubs his palm over his scruffy face that is damn near grown out as mine. "These people aren't your old high school buddies experimenting. This is a married couple with a past. They, at some point, deeply loved each other. I'll say it again, man, it's not right."

"Yeah, I guess," I say with a huff.

"Have you considered switching out of your class and quitting your job?" he asks.

Irritation flits through me. "I've considered it."

"But?" Frustration is written all over his features.

"But I'm too selfish."

He lets out a heavy, resigned sigh. "You're going to have to make your own mistakes. Nobody, not even me, can steer you in the right way if you're hell-bent on going where you want. I've warned you of the risks. All I can do is trust you'll use good judgment and think things through before you act. Consider the ripple effects of every look, every gesture, every action. Each dip into their marriage will ripple the waters tremendously. I know you like them, but sometimes it's not about you. It's about what's right."

"What if they both want it?" I argue.

"It's up to you to tell them no. Seriously, it can't end well."

He's right. It pisses me off, but he's right. That's the reason I pushed them together the night we all kissed. They willingly went off together, leaving me alone on that couch. As it should be. They're fragile and if I do anything to disrupt that, they'll break for good. I don't want that shit on my shoulders.

"Fine, Preach. I got it. Stay away from the married couple," I grumble.

Relief flashes in his eyes. "Thank you. Now let's get over to Steph's because she promised me slow-cooked ribs. I'm eating for two now."

I start laughing. "You knocked Lacy up again?"

"We're trying." The good preacher's grin is devilish. "She looked real good carrying my son. I can't wait to see her big and pregnant again."

Chapter
ELEVEN

Vaughn
Three weeks later...

"He'll be right with you, Mr. Young," the receptionist says from the office doorway as I take a seat.

I grit my teeth and give her a clipped nod. I'm still twitching from the three cups of coffee I've already had this morning and it's not even eight yet.

This is a mistake.

Get up and go.

But it's not a mistake. We've tried and tried. And just when I have hope of us fixing what's broken, we drift back apart. Fuck. I rub at the tension at the base of my neck and will the stress to go away. It won't go away, though. When I think about a future without Vale, it feels empty. Yet when I try to think about us going at the rate we are, I realize we're both fucking miserable.

How do we find that love again?

The love that had me head over fucking heels for her a decade ago. I used to worship her—her body, her mind, her soul. Now, that queen I vowed to love and adore 'til death do us part, has stepped down from her pedestal. I feel lost without her there.

"Vaughn," Dane Alexander, my friend and divorce attorney, greets as he strides in. He's about ten years older than me, but he's clearly been hitting the gym. I'd met him at a gala for the university before Vale and I were a thing. Despite him having a wife at the time, I'd seen his appreciation of myself in a tuxedo. I'd thought he was hot too. Instead of pushing at that mutual attraction, we became friends. "You're really here."

I frown and give him a nod as he sits across from me at his desk. "I don't have tons of time. You got it ready?"

His brows furl together as he studies me. "Are you sure you want to do this?"

My mind drifts to last night.

"Your mind is elsewhere," Vale says, a sob catching in her throat. "You're going through the motions."

I stop thrusting to look at her. Her green eyes have lost their luster. She's empty inside. Well, aside from me being balls deep in her cunt.

"I'm fucking my wife," I snap a little too harshly. "Where else would I be?"

Her eyes grow teary and she looks away. "Are you thinking about him?"

Gritting my teeth, I slide out of her, my cock softening at this "discussion" in the middle of sex. "Are you thinking about him?"

She refuses to meet my gaze, but the blush creeping up her throat is her tell. Once again, we dance around our feelings and truths.

"Vale," I say softly. "We need to—"

"I'm tired. So tired." Her teary eyes meet mine. I don't miss the underlying message. She's tired of me. Of us.

"Go to sleep," I urge, desperation bleeding into my tone. Hearing her intent guts me.

"Not that kind of tired," she whispers. "Tired of everything."

Leaning in, I kiss her mouth, but she doesn't kiss me back. My cock is completely soft now. Rejection will *do that to a man.*

"I'm going to sleep on the couch," *I mutter.* "So you can rest."

Beg me to stay.

Fucking please, Vale.

"Okay."

Okay.

We're fucked.

This is the end.

"Vaughn, buddy," Dane says, bringing me to the present. "I can toss it in the shred right now."

I stare at the divorce papers tucked away in a big yellow envelope and labeled YOUNG. Reaching across the desk, I pull it to me. "This has been a long time coming. For nearly a year now."

He lets out a sigh. "You should think about it a little more. Have you considered counseling? I have a friend, Easton McAvoy, and he could—"

Waving him off, I shake my head. "It's over, man. Thank you for this."

As I rise, he eyes me warily. "Take care."

The ride to campus, I'm numb. Completely in a

zone. When I park, I climb out with the divorce papers in my grip. I stalk into the building and make a beeline to my office. I have a couple of Aiden's assignments to grade since he's my TA and can't grade his own shit, including last week's test, before I go to class this morning. But as I stomp into my office and sit down, I'm not ready to grade papers.

I pull out the documents and read through them. So harsh. Black and white. A division of two people. An ache forms in my chest and I swallow to try and ease it.

"Vale, what have we done?" I mutter, running my thumb over her name.

Anger surges through me and I shove it away. I pull out Aiden's test and start grading to take my mind off my life. Problem is, I find myself fond of his handwriting. Messy scribbles that just seem so him. I'm fascinated by his words until I realize his essay answers are all bullshit. Stuff he made up, talking out of his ass, rather than the real answers. He's not even close to the right answers. On any of them. By the time I make it to the end and he earns a whopping 27 percent on his exam, I'm completely livid. What's his fucking deal?

Rising to my feet, I check my watch and realize

I'm running out of time. I snag his papers along with the others he already graded for me and stalk down to the auditorium classroom. When I step inside, a few guys wince my way. A few girls giggle. I walk straight to the podium, depositing everyone but Aiden's tests, and look for him.

He's sitting in the front row, two girls standing in front of him talking, as he texts someone. A surge of fiery anger bursts up inside me. Is he texting my wife? Are they planning a whirlwind romance the moment I'm out of the fucking picture?

I almost convince myself that's it, but then I remember she has no clue I'm about to serve her with divorce papers.

Fuck.

His eyes lift to meet mine and the steel in his gaze is gone. Soft grayish blue as he regards me with such a longing, I can feel it in my gut. It makes me want to walk over to him, drag him out of his seat, and kiss the hell out of him until he's smiling against my lips.

"Miss Stevens, can you pass out the tests?" I ask one of the girls nearby, my gaze never leaving his.

"Yes, sir," she chirps, bouncing over to the podium.

I prowl over to Aiden and his jaw clenches. His

dulled eyes flare to life as I near. It satisfies me when his nostrils flare and he bites the inside corner of his lip. I want to bite it too.

No.

I want to bitch him the fuck out over his test.

Slapping his test down, I leave my hand planted on his desk and get near his face. "You failed," I hiss, low enough for only him to hear.

He snorts. "I figured."

I want to grab him up and fucking throttle him. "It's unacceptable."

"Why do you care?" he mutters.

"I just do," I snap back.

All he does is shrug.

"My office. After class."

He smirks but gives me a nod. I'm nearly shaking with fury by the time I make it to the podium. Everyone is quiet as they look over their tests. I suppose they can sense I'm about to blow a gasket. Somehow, I manage to avoid looking at Aiden and make it through the lecture without killing anyone. When class is over, I snatch my shit up and stomp away from the room. As soon as I'm in my office and deposit my things on the desk, I rub at the tension on the back of my neck.

The sounds of people walking in the hallway are muted when someone steps in and closes the door. Heat seems to cloud around me, letting me know it's Aiden. He's the only one who has this effect on me. I turn and glower at him.

"What the hell, Aiden?"

His brows furrow and he looks out the window. "I just flaked out."

I dart over to him until we're just inches apart. "You can't just flake out. You'll fail my class."

His eyes flip back to mine and emotion flares in them. "I'm just not in the mood for school."

"It doesn't fucking matter," I snap. "You do it anyway."

"Jesus," he grumbles. "You really do sound like my dad."

He steps away from me and walks over to my desk, his arms crossed in front of him with his back to me.

"What's going on?" I ask, softer.

"I'm going through some shit."

"Want to talk about it?"

He shakes his head. "Part of that shit involves you."

I wince because I know what he means. Vale and

I both made out with him and then pushed him away to work on our marriage. That kind of rejection, doubly so, has to hurt.

"We should go for coffee. Talk about it," I suggest. Just the idea of spending more time with him outside of class has my heart thudding in my chest. It makes me think of the last time we spent time outside of class. When we made out in a bar bathroom and it was hot as fuck.

"What the hell is this?" Aiden hisses, his voice icy, chilling all heated memories out of my mind.

"What?"

He turns and holds up the divorce papers. "This."

Shame burns up inside me. "None of your business."

"You're really doing it?" he growls. "Really fucking doing it? What? Vale not good enough for you anymore?"

"You know there's more to it than that," I bite back, fisting my hands.

He tosses the papers onto my desk and rushes over to me, his chest bumping mine. "More to it, huh? Care to explain?"

"We're broken," I utter, my chest squeezing at that thought.

"So you fucking fix it," he roars, shoving me. "You fix what's broken because it's worth it."

He goes to shove me back and I grab hold of his hoodie, slamming his back into the door. "I can't fix, goddammit! If I knew how, I would've done it months and months ago." My voice cracks at my admission.

His gaze softens. "She'll be brokenhearted."

My throat tightens as I rasp out, "*I'm* brokenhearted."

"Don't give up," he pleads.

Why? Why does he fight for this so hard? He's clearly attracted to us both. He could get what he wants by our relationship's demise.

"We're too broken," I whisper.

His eyes watch my lips and then they're fiery as he glares at me. "So you fix it."

"Relationships don't work like that. It's not like a little glue will put it all back together and make it pretty again. It's ugly, Aiden. It gets uglier each day." My bitterness bleeds into my tone.

"See someone. Talk to someone. Don't give up," he begs.

"Why do you care so much?" I demand.

"You know why." His brows furl together. "Because I want you both to be happy."

"I'm happy right now," I mutter, my voice husky.

Our eyes meet and his are burning with lust. I step closer, rubbing my aching cock against his through his jeans. He groans and his hips rock with mine.

"You can't be happy with me," he explains in a deep, rough voice.

I release his hoodie to slide my palms up his hard chest to his neck. "I think I can."

My lips press to his and at first, he remains motionless. Then, with a small moan, he opens his mouth and accepts my kiss. I swipe my tongue across his and both of our dicks jerk in response.

"I don't want to be the one who divides you," he rasps between kisses.

I bite his bottom lip, loving the sounds of pleasure vibrating through him. "We've been divided for a long time, Aiden." I slide my hand to the front of his jeans and palm his thick, hard cock through the material. "I've had a shit day and I really want to feel good. With you. Let me touch you."

"When you look at me like you want to fucking devour me, it's kind of hard to say no," he grumbles. His lips turn up on one corner.

"Good," I growl. "I like it when you say yes."

He hisses when I start fumbling at his belt. Within

seconds, I shove his jeans down his thighs and grip his dick through his boxers. Such a sexy as fuck sound erupts from him when I push my hand into his boxers to touch his cock. Goddamn, he's hung. Thoughts of taking him in my mouth have pre-cum leaking from my dick. He's hot as hell and I'm sinning like a motherfucker with him.

"I like your cock," I mutter against his mouth, biting at his lip again. "I like it a lot."

He chuckles, the sound dark and devious. "It likes you too. Fuck if I'm not about to come like a little bitch."

I fist him in a slow, teasing way. His hips rock desperately against my hand.

"I want to touch you too," he tells me, his voice low and husky.

My eyes close when he begins undoing my slacks. With the weight of my belt on my slacks, the pants fall to the floor quickly. He shoves down my boxer briefs and then his large, powerful hand is gripping me like I grip him.

Fuck.

Fuck.

"This feels good," I moan, eager for each stroke he gifts me. "So fucking good."

"And long overdue," he murmurs.

We crash our mouths together for a desperate, needy kiss. Each of us is trying to inhale the other. His taste is so fucking addictive.

"Let me see your hand," he murmurs against my mouth. "I saw this on Tumblr and I want to try it."

I look down between us as he pulls me closer and and then helps me wrap my hand around the base of both our cocks so that they're parallel, pushed against the other. Then, he mimics my action but up toward the tips. Our eyes latch onto each other as we both stroke together. Up and down. Squeeze and release. Over and over again. Our grunts and hisses are in tandem as we both climb higher and higher.

With his free hand, he yanks off his hoodie and T-shirt all at once, revealing his tanned, toned abs. The dark trail of hair to his impressive dick is something I will run my tongue along one day. Fuck, he's hot.

"That's it, Professor," he growls. "Make us come all over my stomach."

"Fuck, you're dirty," I groan, bucking my hips against our hands and his cock.

"You haven't seen just how dirty I can be," he tells me, a wolfish grin on his handsome face.

Goddamn, I want to run my tongue along every

surface of him. He's that fucking delicious looking.

"Look at these fat cocks ready to explode," he rasps. "We're going to make a mess."

His words have me struggling to stay sane. My balls tighten. "I'm going to come soon."

"Do it," he orders. "I want to see your cum mixed with mine."

That sends me over the edge and my nuts seize up. Cum shoots straight into the air and then another spurt lands across his lower abdomen. He lets out a groan as my cum coats our dicks and lubes them up. His own release shoots out thicker and more plentiful. It squirts up his chest, wetting his pecs. We're both breathing heavily as our cocks stop soaking him and our hands.

"Holy shit," I groan. "That was hot."

"Did you have any doubts, Professor?" He lifts a brow, smirking at me. "Because I had none whatsoever."

"I knew it would be good," I admit with a grin. "Didn't know it'd be that good. And if you keep calling me Professor, I may have to push you to your knees and give you a lesson on cleaning my cock."

Someone knocks on the door and tries to push in but thank fuck Aiden is stronger and pushes back.

"Mr. Young," a young woman chirps. "I had a

question about my test. Do you have a moment?"

I clear my throat as I reach over for the tissue box. "I do," I clip out. "I'm with another student. Give me five minutes."

"Okay," she says and stops trying to push inside.

Aiden and I quickly clean up. I've already re-dressed and am squirting hand sanitizer on my palms before he even has a chance to pull up his jeans. I take a moment to admire his physique. Oh, to be eighteen again. Goddamn, he looks good. He catches me staring as he pulls up his boxers and winks at me.

And my dick is jolting in my slacks.

He flexes his abs that still glisten with missed cum. This guy is going to make me lose my mind. He throws on his shirt and then pulls on his hoodie before stalking over to me. His lips crash to mine again, causing heat to burn through me.

"Aiden," I murmur. "We have to stop."

"We'll pick this up later," he tells me, confidence dripping in his tone. "And, Vaughn?"

"Yeah?"

"Tear it up."

He pulls away and his heated eyes are filled with concern.

"Your test?"

"No," he says with a heavy sigh. "The divorce papers."

I scowl at him. "It's done."

"It's not fucking done," he argues. "Give it more time."

"Way to convince me, man," I say bitterly. "You just rocked my goddamn world and now you're telling me I should stay with my wife. Doesn't make a lick of sense."

He grips my jaw and runs his thumb along my bottom lip. "Let me help."

"Aiden…"

"Mr. Young," the girl calls out again. "I can come back if it'll be a while."

Aiden gives me a hard look that says we'll be discussing this more later before pulling away. Where his hand was, I can still feel the burn. He opens the door and grins at the brunette.

"Hey, Nora," he greets. "We're done here. He's all yours."

Her cheeks burn red. Under Aiden's intense stare, it happens to the best of us.

"We'll talk later," I call out.

Aiden winks at me.

Goddamn this man.

Chapter

TWELVE

Vale

"**D**onuts. You definitely need donuts and this place will be perfect," Sheriff McMahon says, sipping his coffee.

His deputy, Gentry, shrugs. "I don't know. Donuts are so last year, Sheriff. Lemon berry muffins are the shit. I'm a fan." He grins at me as he bites down on the fresh muffin.

I beam at them, happy to have new customers. "I'll look into donuts," I tell the sheriff. "But the muffins are here to stay. I'm trying to make the shop better and bring in new customers. If donuts will do it, then I'll start making donuts."

The sheriff sips his coffee and drags his gaze over every surface in the shop. I feel exposed under his scrutiny. My little shop saw like ten customers a week before Aiden started helping me. Now, all these people are checking it out and making critiques. It's both exciting and nerve-wracking.

"My wife would like this place," he says. "She's recently started blogging with my daughter. It's mostly a mom blog where they take pictures of the babies and their outfits, but they've been doing a lot of food and other stuff."

"Jessie calls it 'foodgramming,'" Gentry offers. "My fiancée is really into that shit."

"Foodgramming?" the sheriff asks, his brows pulled together. "What sort of dumbass name is that?"

"It's a thing," Gentry argues. "Look it up, old man."

"Old?" he huffs. "I think you forget who can outbench you at the gym. What's your time on the mile? That's right. Not even close to mine. Take your big mouth, muffin eating, young ass somewhere else and let the adults talk."

I crack up laughing. The men are both gorgeous as hell and funny. It's nice having customers, especially good-looking ones. "I think it all stems from Instagram," I explain to the sheriff. "My friend Aiden says if we want customers I need to take pictures and put it on Instagram. I forget my login half the time, much less remember to do it every day."

The sheriff chuckles. "Aiden Blakely?"

A blush creeps up my neck. "Yeah. You know him?"

"It sounds like you hit a gold mine if you have a Blakely helping you with marketing and advertising. Don't let that one go," he says, grinning at me. "He's a good one."

My pervy ass is on a totally different page than the sheriff. In my head, I'm holding onto him for completely different reasons than marketing. Those images are of us together in bed. Naked. Up to all kinds of no good. The same images I got myself off to three times this week. Now, my neck is really burning.

Gentry shakes his head. "I don't think she plans on letting Aiden go."

The sheriff frowns as understanding washes over him. "What? Aiden? He's just a kid."

"I'm married," I say a little harshly.

They ignore me as they continue talking.

"Just a kid?" Gentry snorts. "That's awfully sanctimonious coming from you, Sheriff."

The sheriff growls. "My wife isn't a kid."

Gentry shrugs. "Just saying she ain't that old either. This town has a thing for youngsters."

"And with that, we're out of here," the sheriff grumbles. "Good luck to you. We'll be back. Just make sure you have some of those muffins ready to fill this knucklehead's big mouth with. He's the town gossip apparently."

I giggle and give them a wave. "Your secrets are safe with me."

The bell chimes and we all glance over. As if speaking of the devil, Aiden walks in, intensity blazing in his eyes. His eyes skim over the two officers and land on me. I squirm under his heated stare.

"Well, if it ain't not-so-little Aiden. We were just talking about you, boy," Gentry says playfully.

Aiden grins at Gentry. "I'm a good subject of conversation. Was it about my ass? Everyone talks about my ass."

The sheriff groans. "No, dumbass. We were talking about instafooding."

Aiden's brows furl together. "What the hell is instafooding?"

"I knew it wasn't a thing," the sheriff barks at Gentry. "I knew you made that shit up."

Gentry snorts. "You caught me." Then, he mouths to me, "Old man."

The sheriff tips his hat at me and then storms

out of the coffee shop with a chuckling Gentry on his heels. As soon as they leave, Aiden turns the lock on the front door before switching the sign to closed.

"What are you doing?" I ask in confusion.

He prowls toward me and I find myself backing up into the back room. It doesn't deter him and he stalks me. When my ass presses against a shelf, he crowds me, his strong body pressing against mine.

I can't breathe.

My heart is racing out of my chest.

Tilting up my head, I bravely look him in his eyes. "What are you doing?" I ask again, my voice breathy.

"What are *you* doing?" he murmurs back, his hot breath mingling with mine.

"I'm smashed against shelves by my employee," I utter.

"Do you like it?"

My core throbs at his words. Of course I like it. He's starred in more fantasies than I can count where we end up just like this in nearly all of them.

"I'm married," I choke out. As if I need to hear the words more than him.

His gaze darkens. "Your marriage is in pieces."

I swallow, tears threatening. "Thanks for the reminder."

He grips my jaw and angles my head up. When his lips descend on mine, I put up no fight. In fact, I part my lips, anticipating a kiss I've only dreamed about lately. His kiss is soft at first, but then he seems to lose himself to hunger. I groan against his mouth as he devours me. He slides his palm down my throat and grips my breast over my apron. I let out a moan of appreciation. Then, his hand slides down my stomach. When he touches my pussy over my leggings, I hiss out a sharp breath.

"Aiden," I cry out.

His mouth kisses a trail to my neck and then his teeth tug at my earlobe. "Yes, beautiful?"

I melt at his husky words. "I…"

"Are you asking me to stop?" he murmurs as he rubs at my clit through my clothes. "Or are you asking me to go?"

My breath hitches and I dig my nails into his hard biceps. "I don't know…"

But when he starts to move his hand, I do know. I know without a shadow of doubt.

"Go," I rasp out.

I feel his smile against my neck. Then, he runs his tongue along my flesh as he tugs at the string of my apron behind me. He pulls it away before bringing his palms to my hips. My leggings and panties get pushed down my thighs. The coolness of the air does nothing to take away the heat burning between my thighs.

I want him so bad.

Oh, God, I want him.

"You want this?" he asks, his voice teasing and playful.

"Yes."

"Are you wet for me, beautiful?"

"So wet."

"I don't believe you," he murmurs as he bites my neck. "I better check for myself."

His fingers slide along my slit, bypassing my throbbing clit, and his longest one pushes inside me.

"Fuck, you're a little truth teller," he groans. "You're dripping wet for me. Soaking my finger, just wishing it were my big cock. Is that right, baby?"

His words coupled with the way he curves his finger inside of me and pushes against my G-spot have me trembling in pleasure. "Y-Yes. I wish it were your cock."

He rubs his thumb on my clit and I cry out, clenching around his finger. "That's it," he whispers hotly against my ear. "Tighten that pretty pussy around my finger. How will you ever take my big cock? You're tight as fuck, Vale."

I groan and shamelessly ride his finger. The juicy sounds my body is making are hot. The whimpers coming from me and the growls rumbling from him are even hotter.

"It'll fit," I choke out.

"Damn right it will," he rumbles. "I'm going to take all your holes. I'm going to stretch them all out because I have a plan."

"Sounds nefarious," I hiss, trembling against his touches.

"So evil, baby. But you're going to love it."

He rubs my clit until I'm shuddering, right on the cusp of ecstasy.

"Aiden!" I cry out.

"Come for me, Vale," he growls, pressing harder against my clit.

I moan loudly as my legs tremble. My vision goes black when my orgasm hits, rocking me to my core. I barely register that he's using his other arm to hold me up because my own two useless legs aren't. As soon as I'm relaxed and sated, he slides his finger from me and helps me stand upright again.

His fiery gaze is on mine as he brings his wet finger to his lips. He parts his full lips and pushes his finger inside his mouth. And just like he fingered me moments before, he mimics the action but inside his mouth. I bite on my bottom lip and stare helplessly at how hot he is doing it. Wickedness gleams in his eyes as he slides his finger back out of his mouth.

"You taste like sugar, sweet Vale."

I smile but then unease clutches my heart. What have I done?

He must sense my impending freak-out because he kisses my mouth gently. "Don't worry," he whispers. "Trust me."

My heart races in my chest. "We shouldn't have done that."

"But we did do that," he says firmly. "And we're going to do it again. Besides, we were just getting even."

I stare at him in confusion. "What?"

"Get out of here, Vale. Take the day to pamper yourself or go shopping. Do something fun just for yourself. Then, go home and have dinner with your husband. Promise me you'll do it," he says, his features hardening.

The very thought of spending time with Vaughn when we can barely manage each other's presence is overwhelming. But I need to come clean to my husband. Admit that we've tried but there is no fixing what's broken. It's time to stop fooling ourselves.

"I promise," I say.

He bends and helps me pull up my leggings and panties. "Good girl. Call me later."

I frown at him in confusion because we don't talk on the phone, just the occasional texts about the schedule and the shop. "Okay…"

He saunters off to the bathroom and I can't help but watch his ass. "See you later."

I spent the day shopping for updated décor for the coffee shop. Found a bunch of sales and a super helpful lady at Pier 1. Turns out some retail therapy was just what the doctor ordered. But as I dump all the bags on the living room floor, reality creeps back in. Vaughn will be home soon and I'll need to confess.

Tonight, it will end.

My stomach clenches and I feel like I might be sick. The room spins as tears burn in my eyes. I don't understand how we got here. And if I love him so much, then why are we so miserable? It's not just him. It's me. Together, we're just so damn depressing.

The back door opens and Vaughn's familiar heavy footsteps thud into the kitchen. His eyes burn into me, but I can't meet his gaze. I clutch onto the counter to keep from collapsing.

This is it.

Say the words.

Admit defeat.

My lips fuse stubbornly together.

He approaches me and when his dress shoes are in my line of sight, I try not to wince.

"Vale?"

Swallowing down my emotion, I lift my chin and meet his stare. I expect anger or irritation. Not heartbreak. No bloodshot eyes and pain bleeding from his features.

"Yeah?" I choke out.

"I, uh, I did some things today." Shame causes his cheeks to turn red and he hangs his head remorsefully. "Things I'm not proud of."

Tears well in my eyes and then streak down my cheeks as I nod. "Me too."

He rubs at the back of his neck. "Fuck, why is this so hard?"

"I don't know," I rasp out.

"I…" He squeezes his eyes shut and lets out a huff

of air. "I fucked around with Aiden."

Relief surges through me and I don't know why. I should be angry with him, but the guilt that was weighing on me doesn't feel so heavy. "Me too," I admit.

His brown eyes are sad as they meet mine. "I filed for divorce."

I let out a sharp breath of air as though I've been punched in the gut. Wrapping my arms around my middle, I try to hold in the pain that has me in its clutches. "You did?"

"I did. And…" He frowns at me. "Aiden was pissed."

"Aiden knows?"

"He does," he says. "We've really been shitty bringing him into our problems."

"We have," I agree. "It's confusing and frustrating to me. I can only imagine how he feels."

"Lonely. Guilty," he utters. "He thinks he's dividing us."

"We were already divided," I assure him. "It's not Aiden's fault."

He steps toward me and takes my hand. Warm and comforting. I want his touch.

"That's what I told him. He wants us to fix things,"

he says, bringing my knuckles to his lips. He kisses them and my heart stutters in my chest. "But, Vale baby, I don't know how. Fuck if I didn't stew about this all damn day. I want to be with you. I don't want to divorce you. Yet I'm not happy. Everything feels so fucked up beyond repair." He stares at me helplessly as though I have all the answers.

I step closer to him and let out a sigh of relief when he hugs me to him. The love that we have trouble finding some days patters back to life. A sob chokes me as I inhale my husband.

"What do we do?" I ask, my tears soaking his dress shirt.

"I think you know."

"It's risky," I breathe. "What happens when it doesn't work?"

He brings his palms to my cheeks and tilts my face up to look at him. "Promise me we'll move on amicably. That we won't try to pull him in our direction. We just let the chips fall where they may. I don't want to hurt him too. It's already bad enough what I've done to you."

"It's not just you," I say fiercely. "I'm fucked up too, Vaughn."

His lips press to mine and I wish I could freeze

the moment. After a soft, sweet kiss, he pulls away to stare at me, his brows pinching together.

"Yes or no?"

"Yes," I say without hesitation. "We try. A last resort. He helped us so much that night. What if he's just the fix we need?"

"Okay then," he says, a smile tugging at his lips. "I have no fucking clue what we're about to do, but I want to try. I'll do anything to save us, Vale. I don't want to give up yet. There's still fight in us."

I kiss his lips again. "I'll call him."

Call me later.

He knew. He knew it would come to this.

Oh, Aiden, I hope we don't break you too.

Chapter

THIRTEEN

Aiden

"We want you to be the glue."

Those were Vale's words when she called earlier and now I'm buzzing with pent-up energy. Can I do this? Will I really be able to help them? What happens when they are fixed again? What happens to me?

I'll walk away.

My gut clenches at that thought, but Easton was right. I don't want to fuck them up. I just want to help them. I like them both. I'm sexually attracted to both. Any time I'm in the room with either of them, the room is thick with tension. They both feel it too, which is why I'm sitting in their driveway about to do something probably fucked up to an outsider.

I'm not an outsider.

I want to be on the inside with them. And they want me too.

Fuck, why do I feel so panicked all of a sudden?

Because I don't want to hurt them or make things worse. I wish I could talk to my dad or Anthony about this, but they'd both freak the fuck out. It's not normal, they'd say. Back the hell up, they'd say. And I don't want to do that.

Which is why I'm climbing out of the car with my overnight bag tossed over my shoulder.

"Bring a bag."

There was no mistaking the intent in those words. They want me to spend the night. And this time, I don't think they want me to sleep on the couch.

I trot across the yard and let myself in the back door. The house smells good and I find them both in the kitchen. At first, they don't notice me. They're both tense but talking about some décor Vale bought at the store today for the shop. For a second, it feels normal and like I'm intruding, but I'm frozen. I drink them both in.

Vale is beautiful in a pair of jeans and an off-the-shoulder sweater. Her reddish brown hair has been twisted into a top knot. I love how having her hair pulled up exposes her lovely, long neck. A neck that would look even more pretty with marks left all over it.

I drag my gaze over to Vaughn. He's long since changed into a pair of sexy jeans and a brown Henley long-sleeved shirt that hugs every muscle. He's fine as fuck. They're the hottest couple I've ever met.

"Smells good," I say, announcing my presence. I'm selfish because I want them to ask me to stay.

Vale turns and flashes me a warm smile. "Vaughn says I make the best chicken parmesan. I think you'll love it."

Vaughn's sharp gaze finds mine and intensity burns in his eyes. I grin at him as I walk over to Vale to hug her. Her tension bleeds from her as I embrace her. Then, I turn around and hug Vaughn too. His grip around me is tight as he whispers, "thank you," into my ear. He releases me and sets to opening a bottle of wine.

I know they're both nervous, just as I am, so I try to distract them.

"What else are we having? Should I make a salad?" I ask Vale.

She nods at the fridge. "Stuff is in there. I chopped it earlier, so all you need to do is toss it."

We all work around each other until the

table is set and we're seated. I dive in and groan in appreciation.

"See why it's my favorite?" Vaughn asks me while flashing Vale an approving grin.

She bats her lashes and waves off the comment. "It's pretty basic."

"It's pretty awesome," I correct. "Did Vaughn tell you I failed my test?"

He grunts and she gasps.

"What? No! Why?" she demands.

I shrug. "I hate college. I failed my English exam too. I haven't gotten my other grades, but I'm flunking all my classes, I bet. My dad is going to be pissed."

"As he should be," Vaughn grumbles. "College is important. You can't just blow it off."

"I tried," I tell him. "Dad asked me to try and I did."

"One semester barely counts for trying," Vaughn admonishes.

"Maybe I'm working you too many hours at the shop," Vale says, her nose scrunching up. "If you need to scale back to study more, I could adjust the schedule and—"

"Yes," Vaughn says at the same time I say, "No."

Her brows lift and I laugh.

"Seriously, no. I love my job. It's not that. I just don't like school." Seriously, I hate it. My last job, when my boss took me back after I'd hurt my wrist, she and I got into an argument about school and hours I could work. She'd said it was part-time so I could focus on my studies. I told her I wasn't going to study. We were both stubborn as hell, but she ultimately held all the cards and fired my ass. Dad thinks I quit to get better hours to work around my college courses.

"Let me tutor you," Vaughn grumbles. "I could help you pull your grades out of the toilet."

"By trying to fuck me over the toilet?" I tease. "Last tutoring session ended with my tongue down your throat."

Vaughn drains his wineglass at my bold words.

"And," I continue, "I felt very rewarded for my bad grade today. Did you tell Vale how you rewarded me?"

He tugs at the collar of his shirt and shoots me a helpless look.

"Tell me," Vale mutters, her voice breathless and curious. "I want to know."

"Yeah, Vaughn, tell her what we did," I urge him. "Then she can tell you what I did with my fingers ear-lier." I flash her a wicked grin.

"Wow," Vaughn grunts. "We're doing this. Just openly talking about it."

I pin them each with a firm stare. "Being open and communicative is the only way this will work. The way you two were before—the wall building and shutting each other out—won't work. The three of us will talk about everything. No secrets."

Relief, surprisingly, flickers in their stares. I wave at Vaughn to continue.

"We got each other off...together," he states. Fire glimmers in his brown eyes at the memory.

"Like you jerked each other off?" Vale asks.

"Kind of," I explain. "But we just pushed our dicks together and jacked off at the same time, gripping both cocks. Make sense?"

"I might need a demonstration," she murmurs.

I throw my head back and laugh, which causes them to laugh too. The tension lessens.

"It was hot," I admit. "We came all over my stomach and made a big fucking mess." I narrow my eyes at her and stare at her perfect, pouty lips. "Had you been there, what would we have done, Vaughn?"

Without missing a beat, Vaughn says, "We would've put you on your knees and had you clean us up."

This time, it's Vale who sucks down her wine.

"Now," I say, grinning, "tell your hot husband how you came all over my finger."

Her cheeks burn bright red as she glances up at Vaughn. He stares at her with burning intensity. He's turned on at our little conversation. Hell, we all are.

"He, uh, we were kissing and then he took off my apron." She bites her lip and closes her eyes as though it embarrasses her to say it out loud.

"Go on, beautiful. Your husband's dick is hard as fuck right now imagining you whimpering and orgasming to my touch. Right, Vaughn?"

"Fucking right," he growls. "Tell me more, baby."

She smiles, oh-so-fucking gorgeous. "He pushed down my pants and fingered me. It felt good. I wanted more."

"She'll get more, right?" I ask Vaughn.

"Hell yes she will," he agrees. "She'll get my finger too."

His smile is broad and he shares it with both of us.

"Hey, Vale, I was thinking today while at the shop, we should paint it. The wallpaper in there is nearly as bad as the curtains you had. I bet Vaughn would help us," I say as I inhale the rest of my food.

"Well, I actually pinned some really nice modern

designs on Pinterest like you showed me. I bought décor that goes with maybe a pale gray or an off white. That would be pretty, right?" she asks.

"Anything's prettier than that flowery shit," I retort with a laugh.

She throws her wadded napkin up at me. "Yeah, yeah. I'm trying."

I rise from the table and take her plate. "I'll do the dishes."

"Can we keep him?" she teases.

I can't ignore how my heart skips a beat at that thought.

One step at a time.

"We should, uh, establish rules," Vale utters, wrapping a beach towel around her.

Vaughn saunters into the room wearing a pair of black swim trunks and looks between us. "What are we doing?"

"Vale wants rules," I tell him. "Are these rules something we can discuss in the hot tub? I'm freezing my ass off in your living room."

"Yes, rules," he grunts in agreement. Then, his

smile is wolfish, aimed toward me. "My trunks fit you well."

"We're practically the same size," I agree and throw Vale a wink to let her know I mean our dicks.

She laughs and pushes past me, tickling my side along the way. "You're too much, Aiden Blakely."

I chase after her into the chilly winter air and hook an arm around her narrow waist. She lets out a squeal as I tug off her towel and climb into the steaming hot tub with her in my arms. I settle into a seating position and keep her in my lap. She's still stiff and nervous, but she'll warm up.

"You forgot the booze," Vaughn grunts. "Some of us need some liquid courage."

He saunters across the yard, not at all impacted by the cold air, with a bottle of alcohol in his grip. I drink in his perfect form as he climbs in with us. His abs are cut, hard and defined, and his V-shaped oblique muscles give a promise to what's beneath his trunks. It's big and impressive. I know from experience. He scoots next to us and our thighs brush against each other.

Vale twists in my lap and stretches her legs across her husband's. I give her an encouraging smile. I've been in a couple of polyamorous encounters, but these two have not. I may be the youngest here, but I do have more experience with the dynamics of such situations.

"Okay, rules," I say to Vale. "Let's hear them."

"No jealousy," she tells Vaughn. "Whatever happens, happens. For this to work, we can't be jealous of each other. We're sharing. Everything."

Vaughn tips back the bottle and swallows a healthy swig. "Good rule, baby. I have one." He hands her the bottle. "No scheduling sex times. If we start scheduling who gets who and when, it's no better than when we were trying for a baby. It should be natural."

She sips the liquor, shudders from the burn, and then nods. "I agree. That sure takes the fun out of it." She takes another sip before handing it back to Vaughn.

"I have a rule," I say, caressing Vale's bare stomach. Her yellow bikini is hot as hell on her curvy body. Soon, I'll enjoy stripping her of it.

"Tell us," she mutters, squirming in my grip.

Vaughn smirks at me, knowing just how much I turn his wife on. And that gets my dick hard.

"I see you both at different times. And during those times, we'll be alone. Just two of us. If we want to kiss or fuck around, I want that to be okay. I don't want to have to worry about the other person left out getting upset. Just like when I'm at my house, I won't feel left out if you two fuck." I glance over at Vaughn. "Okay?"

He nods. "I am fine with that."

"Me too," Vale says.

"But we can share details with each other," I tell them, grinning wickedly. "Because that's hot and I sure as hell want to hear about how hard you fuck your wife, Vaughn."

His brown eyes darken. "Is that all? Are we done with the rules because I'm ready to play."

I thread my fingers in Vale's right hand and then reach over to squeeze Vaughn's thigh. "One more thing."

He nods for me to continue.

"I want more than sex," I mutter, my voice soft and vulnerable. "I want a real relationship. With the both of you. Dinner, dates, all of it. We can start slow, but I'm not the type of guy who just fucks and runs. I'm not wired that way. I get attached."

It could be a deal breaker, but I can't not say it.

"We want you for more than sex," Vale assures me. "Right, Vaughn?"

"Absolutely," he growls.

Chapter
FOURTEEN

Vaughn

They both watch me with wide eyes. Burning with lust and anticipation. Each pair of eyes looks at me to start things. I begin with what I know and run my thumb over Vale's nipple through her swimsuit beneath the water. She bites on her fat bottom lip and it makes my aching cock twitch in excitement.

"Take her top off, Aiden," I instruct, my voice husky. "I want you to see my wife's pretty tits. They're perfect."

She blushes and bats her lashes at me. Like she used to when we were first dating.

Aiden reaches up and unties the top. Then, he undoes the bottom part. Soon, the material falls away, leaving her naked from the waist up.

"Touch them," I instruct.

Aiden is compliant and palms both her breasts, with his heated stare on me. He nuzzles his nose against her ear and whispers something that has her head falling back. I rub at my cock, seeking relief because seeing him touch her makes me hard as fuck.

"They're perfect," he agrees, nipping at her earlobe.

His flesh is tan against her pale skin and his large hands cover each of her full tits just beneath the hot water. He pinches her nipples and she squirms.

I rest on one knee and slide my fingers into her messy hair. Her green eyes burn with intensity as I descend my mouth upon her perfect, pouty lips.

"You good?" I murmur against her mouth.

"Yes," she breathes. "You?"

I give her a nod and then speak to Aiden. "You good?"

"Absolutely," he rumbles, his voice thick with need.

"If things get out of hand, all you have to do is say stop. Either of you," I tell them both.

"*Stop* talking and kiss me," Vale teases.

I smile as I kiss her. It starts out sweet, but then her kiss becomes desperate. When she starts moaning,

I wonder if Aiden has allowed his hands to roam elsewhere. The idea of him touching my wife's cunt has my dick straining against my trunks.

"Pull his dick out, baby," Aiden instructs.

Vale's small, eager hands fumble at my trunks. She manages to push them down and then grips me like she does so well. I moan into her mouth. Up and down, she strokes me, squeezing my shaft in a way that has me groaning with need.

"Sit on the edge," Aiden tells me. "I want to watch her suck you."

I rise out of the water, my dick bobbing out eagerly, and sit on the edge. I part my thighs and watch as my beautiful half-naked wife comes between my legs. Her puffy lips are swollen and red from our kiss. I can't wait to see them wrapped around my dick.

"The way he looks at you, baby, is hot as fuck," he tells Vale. "You see that hungry desperation in his eyes?"

She looks over her shoulder at him and then turns to smile at me. "You want me?" Her brow arches in question and her tits bounce as she approaches.

I greedily drink in the way her tits look with water running down each of them. I want to lick away every drop. "Fuck yes, I want you."

She beams at me and her eyes lighten. It's a look I haven't seen on her in years. Pride at causing that look squashes any guilt I have for not making her do it in so long. She reaches for my dick again and this time her tongue is what drives me wild. Soft and unsure at first as she licks the tip, but then she lets out a hungry moan as she starts sliding down over me.

"I've got to say," Aiden growls. "This is the hottest thing I've ever seen." His eyes burning with lust and adoration lock with mine. I rake my gaze over his sculpted chest and hope he has the same sense of appreciation when he sees my body. I'm much older than him, but I do try to keep in shape. I'll never be eighteen again, but there's something to be said about a little age under your belt.

"Are you going to fuck her?" I ask, groaning when Vale gags on my cock. Automatically, my fingers thread into her hair and tighten around her locks.

"Yep. Not right now, though. Right now, I'm going to play with her pussy. You're going to watch," he tells me.

My dick jolts in her mouth and she hums in appreciation.

He sets to untying her bottoms and then tosses them away. His hungry gaze is lazy as he admires the globe of her curvy ass.

"Vale," he rumbles, "we're going to take you together one day soon."

She whimpers around my cock and looks up at me in question.

"Don't worry, sweetheart," I assure her, through my raspy panting, "we'll take care of you. It'll feel good. We'll work up to it."

He grips her ass and pulls it apart. "I bet her ass feels good."

"Really good," I assure him.

His hot gaze darts to mine. "I bet yours feels good too."

My eyes snap closed when she gags on me again. I refrain from holding her down and coming down her throat right then. Fuck, she's making me lose control.

"I haven't done that since before marriage," I choke out.

She moans around my dick and I glance up to see he's fingerfucking her from behind with one hand and stroking his fingertips down her spine with the other. My gaze falls to his full lips that are parted and just begging to be kissed.

"Don't worry," he murmurs, his hot eyes pinning me. "I'll make it feel good. You can fuck me too. I like it. I've been thinking about it a lot. Have you been thinking about it too?"

Vale chokes on my dick again and I nearly come.

"Fuck, Vale," I groan. "You're killing me."

I feel her smile around my cock and it makes my heart speed up. My eyes dart back up to Aiden, who's staring intently at me. The muscles in his forearm and bicep flex as he fingers my wife in ways that have her squirming and moaning. Jesus, this is hot.

"I think about being inside you while you're inside her," I hiss out. "I think about watching you fuck her. I think about her watching me fuck you. I think about your big cock stretching out her tight ass while she rides me. I think about a lot."

He leans forward, his free hand coming to cup around the back of my neck, and pulls me to him. His mouth attacks mine and I lose all sense of control. With Vale sucking my dick and Aiden sucking my tongue, I'm lost to the madness of pleasure. A garbled groan rattles from me as my nuts seize up. Vale, familiar with my tells, eagerly pumps me harder and fuses her fat lips to my dick. Aiden doesn't ease up on our kiss and devours me. Her whimpers tell me he's playing her pussy just like she likes it.

"Fuck!" I bark out as I come. I tilt my head back in

pleasure, breaking Aiden's kiss. His lips find my neck and he sucks me in a possessive way that adds to my climax. My dick drains its release into Vale's throat and my greedy wife gulps it down. It's been so long that she's sucked and swallowed. I'm dizzy from pleasure when she pulls away.

"Come here," Aiden orders, turning her around and pulling her naked body to him. His palms grip her ass and then his mouth is on hers. She clings to his chest as he kisses her wildly. I can only stare at them, smiling as my softening dick thumps back to life. "She tastes so fucking good," he growls. "I can taste your salty cum on her tongue. And she's so sweet. I love it."

He lifts her so her legs wrap around him. Gripping her ass, he uses her to grind over his shaft through his shorts. She moans and wiggles, desperate for relief. I kick out of my trunks and walk over to them. I suck on my middle finger and then I slide it along her ass crack, loving the way she jolts in surprise. When I push against her asshole, she whimpers. I lean in and nuzzle against her wet hair, kissing the side of her neck.

"Let me in, wifey."

She relaxes and I'm able to push my finger into her ass. We've done anal plenty of times. It's just been a while. But, like riding a bike, my wife hops back on as if she never missed a day.

He kisses her roughly and continues to use her body to rub against hers while I finger her ass. It doesn't take long to work her into a frenzy. When she screams loud enough to disturb our neighbors, I chuckle but don't give her any relief. She writhes and spasms until her orgasm has run dry. Then, she melts in Aiden's arms.

I slip my finger from her ass and kiss her shoulder. Then, I kiss Aiden once he breaks free from her mouth.

"Let's move this party upstairs."

We're shivering from the cold when we run inside. Kind of puts a damper on how hot things were getting. But Vale improvises and turns on our shower. We've both been in there plenty of times, but this is the first time we're inviting a third. We'll fit, but it'll be close.

Vale and I both sneak looks over at Aiden since he's the only one not naked. The smug bastard flashes us an easy, arrogant grin before pushing his trunks to his ankles. His dick springs out and I find myself once again admiring his sharp oblique muscles that seem to accentuate his proud cock.

"He has a nice cock," I tell Vale, slapping her ass.

"I'm not the only one with a nice cock," Aiden says as he walks into the shower.

Vale follows after him and I get in next. We sandwich her in. She looks up at him and bites his jaw before looking over her shoulder at me. Her hooded eyes blink lazily at me, inviting me in with her seductive temptress stare that hooked me all those years ago. She's a natural at seducing a man. I'd preferred males over females when I'd met her and something about her just lured me to her.

I grip her hips, twisting her, and push her back against Aiden's front. My now-hard dick presses against her stomach as I lean my head down to kiss her. Aiden reaches around her to grip my ass, forcing me to grind against her. I peel my lips from hers and then seek his mouth above her. We kiss until I want to taste her again and then my mouth is back on hers. The shower is a waste as we don't clean ourselves, only work to get ourselves hotter.

When my dick is lurching with the need to fuck, I pull away from them. "Out. Now. I'm about to go crazy."

Aiden flashes me a wolfish grin. "Lead the way, Professor."

My flesh heats at him calling me Professor. There's a forbidden feel to wanting to fuck my student.

"Your husband's waiting, boss," he says playfully to Vale and slaps her ass, making her squeal.

We quickly dry off and then I grab Vale's hand, bringing her to the bed. I palm her cheeks and rest my forehead to hers.

"Still okay?"

"Yes," she breathes. "I want this. Don't you?"

"More than anything."

Aiden starts opening drawers and I can't help but smile. He's just making himself at home. "I still want to do it too. Not that anyone asked," he teases.

We both turn to look at him. I'd say he was offended except he's grinning at us like that cat that ate the canary holding a bottle of lube.

"Don't look so eager," I grunt, smiling.

His smile widens. "I'm about to fuck the two people I've been obsessing over for weeks. I'm fucking ecstatic."

Vale giggles. "I'm pretty excited too."

"Then let's get this started, beautiful. Put your hands right there on the edge of the bed and let's see that perfect ass," he orders.

She sways those curvy hips of hers and obeys

him. As soon as her ass is prone and ready, Aiden strokes his cock while he admires the view.

"What do you want to do?" I ask.

"I want to fuck her," he says without hesitation. Then, his eyes burn into me. "While you fuck me."

My dick twitches with need. We're really doing this. He's going to fuck my wife and I'm going to fuck him.

He smirks at me before tossing me a condom. I roll mine on and then watch as he does the same.

"Here," he says, handing me the lube. "You'll need this."

My hand has a slight tremble to it as I take the bottle from him. I'm nervous and I don't know why. It's not like I've never fucked a man before. I quite enjoy it. I just worry that maybe I won't be as good as I used to be or some shit.

"You may as well wipe that look off your face, Vaughn," he barks out, jolting me from my thoughts. "Whatever you think is wrong. I'm going to enjoy this. I want this."

Swallowing, I give him a nod of thanks. He winks at me before turning to grip my wife's hip. With slow, teasing motions, he rubs his sheathed cock between her pussy lips until she's whining and pressing her ass back. He chuckles and then slides into her wet pussy. I know it's wet by the way he easily glides inside her.

"Goddammit, Vale," he groans, his control slipping. "I knew you'd feel good but not this good. Best pussy I've ever had."

She moans and her fingers clutch the bedspread as he thrusts into her.

"Touch your clit," I growl out to her. "Show him how crazed with need you get when you get fucked from behind like this."

She throws me a wild-eyed stare that makes my dick ache. Fuck, she's hot. I squirt the lube on my dick and spread it around all over my length. Then, I approach the ass I've thought about for far too long. His muscles clench with each thrust into my wife.

"You ready?" I ask huskily as my lubed fingers tease his ass crack.

He lets out a harsh breath. "Hell yeah."

I push my finger against the tight ring of his asshole and he groans. His thrusting into Vale slows as he allows me to prime his ass to take my dick. Once I've worked him good, I push another finger inside him. He's going to feel so good around my dick.

Slipping my fingers out, I grip my cock and then press my tip against his hole. He groans again when I begin pushing into him. His ass feels so fucking good swallowing me whole little by little. When I slide all the way into him, I run my palm down his spine in an almost reverent way.

"You can fuck me sweet later," he teases. "But I want you to take what we've both been wanting."

A growl rumbles from me and I slap his ass in a punishing way that has him clenching around me. Vale giggles until Aiden slams his hips against her hard. It pulls him away from my dick until he almost slips off me. I dig my fingers into his hip and drive into him. At first, our rhythm is uncoordinated and messy, but soon we find that if we time our thrusts right, it works really well.

"Fuckfuckfuckfuck," Aiden chants in a raspy tone.

I grin as I push into him harder. His ass is tight and it takes everything in me not to come right away. Vale is losing her mind beneath us, especially now that Aiden has pushed her hand away from her clit to take over. The grunts and moans and skin slapping is so fucking hot. I lose myself to the moment of it all, giving myself over to the pleasure.

"Oh God," Vale cries out, just as her orgasm starts off a chain reaction. She trembles and yells as she loses it.

This sets Aiden off because he stiffens against her, his own release escaping. And the moment his ass tightens, it forces my nuts to seize up, expelling a soul-shattering climax from me.

My thrusts slow, but my breathing remains ragged and wild. When my dick begins to soften, I slide out of him slowly. He lets out a hiss at my loss while I stare at his ass that gapes for a moment before closing shut. Then, he pulls out of my wife and shoots me a wicked grin. She collapses on the bed and starts laughing like a madwoman.

"Well, that was fucking amazing," Aiden says cheerfully as he pulls the condom off his dick. He walks over to me and pulls mine off too. "Right, man?"

I kiss his taunting mouth and grin at him. "Hell yeah. You fucked Vale right out of words."

"Good," she mutters against the blanket. "So good." She holds up a thumbs-up, giggling.

"Good but not great?" Aiden teases as he walks toward the bathroom to get rid of the condoms. "Good thing that was just a practice round."

Chapter
FIFTEEN

Vale

I wake to Vaughn's morning wood pressed against my ass. But the moment I stiffen in response, a strong, unfamiliar arm tightens around my stomach.

"Morning, beautiful."

Aiden.

The night before floods through my mind. He fucked me while my husband fucked him. And then, after another shower, they both took turns fucking me. I've never come so much in my life.

But now?

Awkwardness washes over me. My flesh heats in embarrassment now that the liquor is no longer burning through my veins.

"Morning," I croak out.

His palm slides up to my bare breast and he cups it, lazily running circles around my nipple with his thumb. My heart races as I try to make sense over what we've done. We invited another person into our bed and liked it. At least *I* liked it. Vaughn is a hard nut to crack. He seemed to be into it last night, but he's always broodier in the mornings.

"You're being weird," Aiden says playfully, pinching my nipple.

"I just woke up," I grumble.

He kisses my shoulder. "Good. I was going to have to spank you if you started regretting last night."

I slide my hand over his and squeeze it. "I don't regret it."

Together, we remain cuddling for another long hour. Usually, Vaughn is up with the sun and out the door. Today, his soft snores calm my erratic heart. I hope he doesn't regret things. Aiden holds me to him quietly. I can tell he's awake, and his mind is working. Turning, I face him and admire his handsome, young face.

"What should we do today?" I ask, running my fingertips along his jaw.

He turns and bites on my fingers gently. "A good day to paint."

"You're going to help me paint the store. For real?"

His grin is wide as his steel-blue eyes twinkle. "For real. Sleeping bear over there is going to help too."

I snort. "Vaughn doesn't paint."

"He's going to paint today."

Aiden leans forward and kisses me sweetly on the nose as his palm caresses my hip. I'm nervous for some reason, but I want to touch him. Sliding my hand between us, I grip his hard cock. It causes heat to flood through me knowing I turn this younger man on. Definitely good for a girl's self-esteem.

"Grab a condom," he instructs, his voice raspy yet commanding.

I grin at him and then reach over to the end table. Tearing open the foil with my teeth, I watch his eyes flicker with need. Then, my eyes never leaving his, I roll the condom on his thickness.

His fingers slide between my pussy lips and he easily works me up. Every so often, he slides his finger inside of me, checking to see how wet I am. When I'm gasping and shaking, he grins and rolls onto his back.

"Get on, beautiful."

I straddle his muscular body and grab his dick. My eyes drift over to Vaughn, who watches me with a scowl. At first I think he's mad, but when he licks his lips, I know it's because he likes what he sees.

"Don't make this weird," Aiden taunts him as his hand slides to my husband's cock.

Vaughn's eyes close and his hips lift as he thrusts against Aiden's fist. I watch the way Aiden strokes Vaughn as I slide on Aiden's length. A hiss of air escapes me as I settle all the way on him.

Vaughn rolls to his side and reaches between my legs. He starts playing with my clit in expert movements as I bounce on Aiden's cock. Aiden trades staring at my tits bouncing to the way pre-cum leaks from Vaughn's tip. Our heaving breathing is all that can be heard. When Vaughn turns his head to kiss Aiden passionately, I lose myself to pleasure. I cry out as my climax rattles through me. Aiden and Vaughn are both grunting hard. When Aiden's cock throbs inside of me, I know he's found his release. And the familiar sounds coming from Vaughn tell me he's coming too. I've barely come down from my high when Aiden pulls me off him and forces me to lie on them both. Vaughn strokes my hair while Aiden threads our fingers together.

"This is nice," I mutter, my breath still heaving.

"Good and nice," Aiden says in a playfully

grumpy tone. "I'm starting to get a complex here."

"I think what my wife means was that was fucking amazing."

"Yep," I say with a giggle. "Exactly that."

I bite on my bottom lip as Aiden stands on his toes on the ladder to reach the ceiling. He's taping it off and I can't help but check out his ass. His jeans hang low on his hips and he's long lost his shirt. We've closed the shop for the day to paint, but painting isn't what I want to do. Not after having him twice last night and once this morning.

"Hand me another roll," he orders to Vaughn.

Vaughn, also shirtless, saunters over to him and extends his arm to hand him the blue tape. The muscles in my husband's bicep flex and my mouth waters to lick him.

How long has it been since I simply wanted to lick the man who gave me his last name?

As if clued into my thoughts, Vaughn winks at me and gives me a grin I remember from our dating days. Boyish and charming. Before a career and a crumbling marriage drained away his happiness.

I frown and look down at my feet. I'm an idiot. I nearly drove him away. Now that Aiden is here, trying new things with us, I'm seeing Vaughn in a light I haven't seen in some time. It's bittersweet. I'm happy but also sad that I almost lost it. It was nearly out of my grasp.

"Hey," a deep, rumbly voice says.

Strong fingers press under my chin and lift. I stare into Vaughn's deep brown eyes that flicker with concern. He probably thinks I'm second-guessing last night and this morning. I'm not. The deliciously sore reminder has tiny thrills shooting through me every few minutes.

"Hey," I say with a forced smile.

His brow lifts. "Fake."

I smirk, this time a real smile tugging at my lips. "Better?"

He nods and then kisses me in a sweet way that has my heart thumping in my chest. "I love you," he murmurs, his eyes locking on mine. "Don't ever doubt that for a second."

His words are so unguarded and earnest that I can't help but believe him. Often, I worried that his love for me had faded. But I feel it now more than ever.

"I love you too."

He kisses me again and then pulls away when Aiden curses. He's dropped the tape and climbs off the ladder to retrieve it. Our gazes follow him and when he catches us watching him, he winks at us, a lazy grin on his lips.

"If I'm going to be doing all the work, you might as well give me something to look at," Aiden says, teasing us.

"Behave," I joke back. "Half the town would witness something they have no business watching."

"As long as you promise to let *me* watch later," Aiden says, grinning.

We spend the next few hours working hard and I'm pleased when my florals and pastels are replaced with modern shades of gray. Aiden has good ideas and points us in the direction of executing them. After we clean up to let the shop dry, we grab a bite to eat and head back to the house.

"I'm going to take a quick shower and then I'll help you load your décor in the car," Aiden says as he strides through the house.

Vaughn starts a pot of coffee and yawns. He took off work today and instead of resting, we worked him hard. He doesn't look put out, though. No, he looks happy.

"Everything feels lighter," I murmur as I pull his creamer from the fridge and hand it to him.

"Like a weight has lifted," he agrees.

I step closer to him. He grips my waist and hauls me against him. I rest my cheek on his chest and he hugs me tight. The gravity of just how close we were to failure has emotion clutching my throat. A sniffle escapes me. Vaughn kisses the top of my head.

"Everything's going to be okay now," he assures me. "I can feel it."

I can feel it too. "I'm glad."

"I'm fucking ecstatic."

We pour our coffee and sit at the kitchen table, chattering about some advertising ideas Aiden suggested. It's comfortable and easy. Like old times. This time yesterday, I would've laughed at the possibility of ever having a moment like this with my husband ever again.

"I'm too old to stay up all night having sex with two hot-ass men," I tease, stifling a yawn.

Vaughn runs his fingers through his messy hair. "And I'm the old man around here. I'm about three seconds from calling a time-out so we can nap."

I giggle as I rise and grab his hand. Together we walk through the house on a hunt for Aiden. When we walk into our room, I bite on my lip to stifle a laugh.

Aiden is passed out, face down and in nothing but a pair of boxers. He almost looks like a kid with his arms sprawled out everywhere.

"Here I thought it was because I was old," Vaughn says chuckling.

"Aww, he's an old soul," I joke back.

I shed my clothes and scoot up next to Aiden. He wakes up just long enough to pull me to him. Then, I feel Vaughn press against my side. My husband's arm and leg are thrown over us both as he tries to cuddle us both. His nose nuzzles in my hair and I feel his smile.

"I love this," I say with a sigh.

"Me too," they both say back.

Chapter

SIXTEEN

Aiden

"**S**how me," I bark into the phone. "I want to see."

It's not fucking fair that I have a shit-ton of studying to do. I'd say to hell with studying and just study my new lovers instead, but someone likes to play daddy when he thinks I'm slipping. It's been a week since I took the dive with Vale and Vaughn, and we've all fallen into an easy routine.

Eat. Sleep. Fuck. Work.

Doesn't leave much time for studying.

Which is why I was banished by the naughty professor to my house so I could get a few hours in without his dick accidentally finding its way into my mouth.

Vale shows up on the Facetime and I can see she's

riding Vaughn. He slides the camera down her front, focusing on the way her tits bounce as she fucks him. My cock is aching in my boxers. I toss my textbook to the floor and slide my palm past the material to grip my dick.

"This is so unfuckingfair," I groan. "I want to be there."

The screen turns back to Vaughn's scowling face. "We want you here too, but someone had to fuck it all up by letting their grades slip."

Goddamn, I love when he gets all growly.

"To hell with school," I grumble. I take the camera down to where I'm stroking my dick. "I'd rather have this in your wife's ass."

She moans in the background as Vaughn hisses.

"Let me see your face," he orders.

His intense eyes are back on mine in the next moment.

"I miss you guys," I tell him. Fuck, I sound like I'm pouting to my own ears. Of course I'm fucking pouting. I could be naked with these two, but I'm at home instead learning about shit I'll never use again in my life.

"We miss you too," Vaughn utters. "I'll see you in class tomorrow."

He turns the camera back to her body and zooms in on the way her pussy makes his rubber-sheathed dick glisten with her juices. It's hot as fuck.

"I'm going to come all over my stomach, assholes," I hiss out.

She cries out and the sounds he's making send me over the edge. My dick spurts out my release, splattering all over my abs. I lie there breathing heavily as I listen to the both of them come too. When they finish, Vale's pretty sex-sated face comes into view.

"If I were there, I'd clean up that mess for you." She licks her sultry lips, doing nothing but driving me crazier.

"Yeah, yeah," I groan.

"Study hard and I'll make it up to you tomorrow when you get to work." She beams at me before turning the camera back to Vaughn.

"I'll call you guys later before bed," I tell them.

Someone pounds on my bedroom door and I nearly drop the phone.

"Gotta go. Bye." I hang up and yank off my shirt to clean up my mess. "Who is it?"

"Dad."

I pick up my jeans from the floor and pull them on before walking over to the door and letting him in.

"Hey," I greet, hoping I'm not flushed looking. "What's up?"

Dad furrows his brows as he inspects me. Then, he travels his gaze over to the textbook on the floor. "Studying?"

"Yep."

"How's school?"

"I fucking hate it," I say with a huff.

His lips press into a firm line as he walks into the room. He picks up the book and sets it on the nightstand. "What's going on with you?" he asks in that no nonsense way of his.

I laugh and shrug. "Same as always."

"But you're seeing someone."

Two someones actually. "Yep."

"What's her name?"

"Vale."

"Pretty name," he says absently. "You know you can tell me anything." His features soften as he regards me.

Not this. I can promise that Dad won't be half as understanding that I'm fucking a married couple as Easton was when I'd first mentioned it. Dad would probably lock me in my room until I'm forty.

"You have your whole life ahead of you, you

know." His brows furl together. "You don't have to… settle."

I groan because he's done this same spiel with my brother. Anthony whined like a little bitch to me about it. Now, I get why. It's fucking embarrassing and annoying. "Dad."

He shrugs. "I'm just saying that you should enjoy yourself in college and—"

"I really like her," I say sharply. And him.

His eyes narrow as he studies my features. "You're just so young."

"Same age as Ava was when you two met," I challenge.

Despite them being happily married, we both know it doesn't help his argument considering it's awfully hypocritical.

"Ava was different. She was mature for her age."

I arch a brow. "I am too, Dad."

He clenches his jaw. "You're still my kid."

"You don't give your other kid a hard time and last I checked, we're the same age."

"Anthony does what he wants," he grunts.

"I'd like to do what I want too."

He walks over to me and pulls me in for a hug. Dad's not really a hugger, so when he gives you one, you take it gladly.

"It's my job to worry about my kids," he says softly. "I'm worried."

We pull away and I smile at him. "I'm the happiest I've ever been," I assure him.

This seems to satisfy him because he grins back, reminding me of my brother. "Then that makes me happy."

"My office," Vaughn barks, scaring a couple of nearby students.

I fake a groan and stalk over to his office. A few girls give me sympathetic smiles along the way. I try not to let on the fact that for two weeks I've been fucking my professor and his wife. Or the fact that he's probably going to either punish me or reward me based on how well I did on the test. Stepping inside, I inhale his unique scent that seems the strongest in here. He follows me in and shuts the door before locking it.

"We're here to talk about your test," he says in one of his growly, authoritative tones that has my dick aching with need in my jeans.

"I could think of better things to talk about," I joke.

His nostrils flare and his jaw clenches. "And what might those better things be?"

"Your cock," I say, raking my gaze down his front.

Now that we've been seeing each other for a couple of weeks, both Vaughn and Vale have lost their nervousness. Both are just as eager as I am to try new things.

His gaze is smoldering as he unzips his pants. He reaches in and tugs out his cock through the opening. It's hot as fuck seeing his long, thick dick protruding from his slacks. I lick my lips.

"My dick isn't what I wanted to talk about," he murmurs as he strokes himself. "Sit down."

With my eyes on his, I bypass the chairs in front of his desk and sit in his leather chair. I swivel in time to find him rounding the desk. I'm eye level with his cock and my mouth waters for him. When I reach forward, he swats my hand away.

"No."

Desire burns through me because he's always so fucking hot when he gets bossy like this.

"What should I be doing, Professor?" I tease, shamelessly rubbing my dick through my jeans.

"Let's talk about your cock for a minute," he mutters. "Show me."

I mimic his actions and pull my dick through the zipper. He assumes a bored expression despite the way fire burns in his brown eyes.

"Nice dick," he says.

"I think you meant fucking amazing," I challenge.

A smile tugs at his lips. "You know what is fucking amazing?"

I frown. "What?"

"Your test, Aiden. You aced it."

"No fucking way."

"Yes way. Now unbutton your pants and push them down. I'm about to reward you."

I lift my brows in question but waste no time pushing my boxers and jeans down past my knees. My naughty professor takes a knee in front of me. Instead of touching me, he starts undoing the knot on his tie. I watch with rapt attention.

"Are we going to fuck?" I ask.

"Later," he assures me. "Right now I'm going to suck your dick for being a good, studious boy."

I laugh and lean back in my chair. "Then by all means, suck me off, old man."

Instead of getting offended, he flashes me a

wicked look. One that promises dirty deviance. I love that look in his eyes. He slides the tie away and then teases my dick with it. When he grabs my balls and ties the tie around them, a quiver of apprehension unfurls inside me.

"It'll feel good," he says.

And since I trust him because he hasn't failed me yet, I nod and relax. He pulls on the ends of the tie hard enough to make my balls slightly uncomfortable. They bulge from how he has them tied up. He curls his fist around each end of the tie and slightly pulls away from my dick, tightening the grip the tie has on my nuts. I'm about to cry "uncle" and make him back off when he leans forward and licks my shaft from the base on the underside all the way to the tip. His fiery eyes meet mine as he tongues the tip, licking away my salty pre-cum.

"Does this hurt?" he growls.

His intensity bores into me. Vaughn can be rough in the sack, but I like it. I like how Mr. Composed becomes savage when he loses control.

"I trust you," I tell him, gripping the arms of the chair.

His eyes flicker with appreciation before his lips slide down over my dick. He keeps my nuts tied up and each time he takes me into his throat, he tightens the hold. It fucking hurts, but it also sends spirals of pleasure shooting through me. I grip his gelled hair, loving that I'm about to mess it the fuck up and buck my hips up. I hiss in pain when he tightens the tie even harder.

He pulls all the way off and tilts his head up, grinning at me. "I think Vale's ready."

Images of the both of us using her tight holes together, has a groan of need rumbling through me. "We're both going to fuck her soon?"

His wolfish grin nearly has me coming. "She's ready."

Leaving me with thoughts of her stretched out and dripping with need for two cocks has me nearly tumbling over the edge of bliss. When his mouth slides back over my dick, I let out a string of curse words. Goddamn, this man drives me mental with pleasure. I grip his hair tighter and force him to take my entire dick. His throat is hot and tight and I'm seconds from exploding. He tightens the tie and I cry out, caught somewhere between pleasure and pain. The way he swallows my dick overshadows the pain and I can feel my balls squeezing with the need to release. With my balls tied tight, it's harder to come. And I'm glad.

Most times, when I feel the need to come, it happens. Right now, he's able to keep me right on the edge. It's maddening and fucking amazing.

"Fuck," I grit out. "Fuck."

I want to come. I want to drain my release down his throat.

He takes me deeper and his saliva runs down my aching balls.

"Fuuuuck," I hiss.

I don't want to come yet. I want to stay just like this with pleasure pulsating through me forever.

With a yank and a garbled, gargling sound as he pushes me all the way down his throat I could possibly go, I explode. My vision turns black as pleasure zaps through my every nerve ending. I'm moaning so loud I'm sure everyfuckingbody can hear and I don't care. My balls throb as my release gushes down this man's throat. Each time he swallows, I shudder wildly. With a feral sound, he slides off my cock as saliva and cum run down his stubbly chin.

"Fuck, you're hot," I complain as if it's truly a bad thing. But it's the best thing. I'm so fucking lucky.

He takes the back of his hand and swipes away the wetness before untying the tie from my balls. I glance down and they're purple and throbbing. "You should study more often. I love rewarding you."

I grin at him. "I'm going to ace every goddamn test if I get a blowjob each time."

"I knew all you needed was a little motivation."

Chapter
SEVENTEEN

Vale

"**A** customer is going to see," I complain as Aiden sucks on my throat.

He laughs and then bites my flesh. "I locked the door."

"No, you didn't."

"I didn't, but we'll hear the bell if they come in."

I give in when his lips find mine again. He has me sitting on the edge of the bathroom sink with my legs spread open. I let out a squeal of horror when he rips my panties off. Like actually tears the fabric and ruins them.

"You owe me new panties," I huff.

His rumbling laughter has my heart rate picking up. "Your birthday is coming up. I'll buy you some pretty panties then."

I bite on my lip as he hurries to get his dick out. Dutifully, he pulls a condom from his pocket and has his dick covered in the next breath. Then, without any fanfare, he slams into me so hard my head thunks against the mirror.

"Oh God," I cry out.

He thrusts hard and his teeth nip at my bottom lip before he kisses me. I moan into his mouth and clutch at his hair as he fucks me into oblivion. The moment he came to work and told me about his blowjob my husband gave him, I was immediately wet. Even now, I can't get the image out of my head of my husband on his knees with Aiden's dick down his throat. A needy mewl whines from me.

"I know what you're thinking about," he taunts. "It felt so fucking good too. I've never come so hard in my life."

I clench around him as my body tightens in anticipation. He slides his fingers down to my clit and starts working me as though he's done it his whole life.

"Tonight we're going to stretch you out good, beautiful. Tonight you get my fat cock in your ass while your husband takes your needy pussy. You've been begging for it for so long. You think you're ready?"

"Yes!" I cry out. "I'm ready."

His lips crash to mine again and he fucks me so hard I know I'll have bruises everywhere. He's not going sweet or soft. No, now he's feral and wild. I love it.

"Oh, God!" My orgasm hits me violently and if it weren't for his tight grip on me, I'd slide right into the floor. This sets him off because he groans and then grinds his hips against me as he comes. We're both breathing heavily and franticly when the door chimes.

"Crap!"

"I'll get it," he mutters, sliding out of me and tossing the condom in the trash. He pulls up his pants and then calls out to the customer. "Be there in a second." I can hear him washing his hands in the back room as I try to sort myself out. I eventually manage to get myself cleaned up and looking presentable. When I exit the bathroom after washing my own hands, I hear Aiden chatting to someone.

Pride.

I can hear it in his tone.

Telling this person all about what a "shithole" my store looked like before he helped. I snort because he's right. I love the way it looks now and we tend to stay fairly busy just from walk-in traffic. I pull my apron back on and walk out of the back room to see who he's happily talking to.

As soon as a familiar pair of eyes locks onto mine, I realize this guy must be his dad. They look just alike. His father is older, sharper, maybe a little meaner. He narrows his eyes upon seeing me. As though he's sizing me up. Immediately, I squirm under his gaze. The timer on the oven is going to go off soon, so I quickly pull the oven mitt on.

"I'm Vale," I greet with a nervous smile.

Aiden flashes me a sweet grin. "Vale, this is my dad, Quinn Blakely. Dad, this is Vale Young."

Quinn reaches over the counter to shake my hand but since my hand is covered with the mitt, I offer him my left hand. He takes it, but his smile falls.

"You're married?" he asks, accusation in his tone.

My jaw practically unhinges as I jerk my hand back. "I am."

Quinn's friendly stare is gone as he turns his murderous glare on his son. Oh, shit. Did Aiden tell him we were seeing each other?

"A word, son," Quinn hisses to Aiden.

My phone buzzes in my pocket. "I, uh, need to take this. Don't mind me." I rush into the kitchen, panicked. As soon as I'm out of sight, they start yelling.

"Hello?" I answer my phone.

"Hey, baby, I thought we could pick up food from that—"

"His dad is here and I think he's pissed," I blurt out.

"Pissed at what?" Vaughn growls.

"He saw my ring and asked if I was married. I think he probably assumes the worst," I say with a whine. "Are you close?"

"I'll be there in two minutes to help straighten things out."

I hang up and am horrified to find Quinn and Aiden in each other's faces.

"I'll do whatever the hell I want, Dad!"

"Not with a married woman, you won't!"

"You don't understand!"

"Aiden, you've fucked up!"

"Just go the hell away!"

They go on and on barking at each other. Thankfully no customers walk in. When the door chimes, I'm relieved to see Vaughn stalking in. His features are furious and protective. Over Aiden. My heart melts as I run over to him. He clutches my hand and together, a unified front, we walk over to them.

"Is there a problem?" Vaughn growls.

Quinn steps aside and sizes us both up. "I think you know there is."

"And I think there is more to the story than you're allowing to be told," my husband says, his voice deceptively low.

"What kind of games are you two playing with my son?" Quinn demands.

Aiden pinches the bridge of his nose and his cheeks burn red from embarrassment.

"We're not playing games," I say softly.

Quinn sneers at me. "You're both fucking my son—a married couple—and you don't think this is some sort of game?"

"I'm falling for them, Dad," Aiden mutters.

Quinn laughs, but it's dark and cold. "Of course you are. You're the bleeding heart in this family. It's in your nature. But this"—he waves to Vaughn and me— "this is a game. You're a game to them, son."

Vaughn's grip tightens around my hand and he grits his teeth so hard I fear he's going to break them. "It's not a game, Mr. Blakely," Vaughn says in a deceptively calm tone. "We're falling for him too."

Quinn snorts and his tone is derisive. "Give me a fucking break. Let me guess. Marriage was failing? Needed a little spice or kink? You call in my son to light a match on things. Everything's burning bright now, right?"

We all stare at him in silence.

"What happens when that burn fades?" he demands coolly. "Where does that leave him?"

"Fuck off, Dad," Aiden snaps as he storms away and pushes out the front door.

Quinn closes his eyes and his brows furl together. He rubs at the back of his neck as though he's frustrated by the entire ordeal.

"Listen," Vaughn starts. "Aiden isn't some toy for us."

Quinn pierces my husband with a nasty glare.

"Maybe we, uh, could have dinner together. Talk some more," I suggest.

Vaughn gives my hand a supportive squeeze.

"This is more than about sex?" Quinn asks, his eyes narrowed.

The sex is great but so are the morning talks. The never-ending affection. The way he makes us laugh.

"Aiden is our happiness," Vaughn says firmly. "Dinner would be great. He's told us a lot about your wife. Ava, right?"

Quinn relaxes. "We have a hard time finding a sitter on short notice, so dinner would have to be at our house. We have small children."

I smile at him. "Aiden's told us all about his siblings. They sound adorable. I hear the twins are a handful."

Quinn's lips twitch as though he might smile at the thought of them. Instead, he purses his lips together and nods. "Tomorrow evening at seven?"

"We'll be there," Vaughn and I both say at once.

Quinn's gaze bounces between the two of us for a long moment before he gives us a clipped nod and stalks out of the building. We follow him to the door but don't step outside. He says something to Aiden that has his son hugging him. I feel like we just dodged a nuclear meltdown.

"I thought I was going to have to kick his ass," Vaughn grumbles.

I chuckle. "Aww, defending our boyfriend's honor. You're so sweet."

He turns his still-feral gaze on me. "Our boyfriend, huh?"

"It sounds better than lover. He's more than a lover."

His lips press to mine. "He's definitely more."

We follow Vaughn in my car to the house. But instead of taking us home, he pulls into one of the busy steakhouses not far from home. Aiden has been quiet despite my probing. I can tell he's still upset about the fight he had with his dad.

"We're going out to eat?" Aiden asks, his brows lifted in surprise. "The three of us?"

Vaughn laughs and tries to ruffle Aiden's hair but gets shoved out of the way.

"Boys," I say with a faux grumble.

"Why wouldn't we all three go out to eat together?" Vaughn asks.

Aiden looks at me and I shrug. "We like food."

Aiden snorts. "I like food too."

"So glad that huge relationship hurdle is over," Vaughn says with a teasing groan. "Don't tell me you're going to order salad but secretly steal my fries."

Aiden, his shoulders relaxing, just chuckles. "You know I can out-eat your big ass."

We walk inside the fancy rustic steakhouse and they take us to a booth near the back. Aiden sits down and I motion with my head to Vaughn. Aiden isn't his normal self and if anyone can pull him out of a funk, it's Vaughn. Vaughn, for the longest time, was the only one who could pull me out of a funk.

Aiden's eyes are wide with surprise when Vaughn sits beside him. I sit across from them and reach over to grab Aiden's hand. He settles and his easygoing grin is back on his handsome face.

The waitress brings us some menus and takes our drink order before leaving us. I smile at Aiden.

"Are you growing a beard?" I ask as I reach across the table to run my fingers through his thickening scruff.

He grips my wrist and turns his head to kiss the inside of my palm before releasing me. "I don't like feeling like the kid in our threesome."

Vaughn snorts and nudges him with his shoulder. "Nothing about the size of your dick or how you use it indicates you're a kid. Hell, you give me a run for my money and I've got a helluva lot more mileage on mine."

"You guys didn't have to take me out to cheer me up," Aiden says, his features turning stormy. "People don't exactly accept what we're doing."

Vaughn shakes his head. "Your dad is just being your dad. Overprotective. I get it. He's worried we're going to hurt you." He hooks an arm over Aiden's shoulders and pulls him to him. "We're definitely not out to hurt you."

The waitress returns and hands out our drinks. Once she takes the order, she leaves us once again. She also never bats an eyelash that Vaughn kept his arm around Aiden.

"I'm sorry my dad was such a dick," Aiden says. His hand reaches across the table again, seeking mine. I grip it and give him a comforting squeeze.

"Stop worrying," I tell him. "It'll be fine. One day at a time."

His smile is both happy and sad at once. Two emotions warring for control. It's a little heartbreaking to see.

"I warned you guys," he says softly, his eyes lingering on me before turning to my husband. "I warned you guys it would be more than sex for me."

Vaughn dips down and kisses his mouth sweetly. "It's always been more than sex for us too. It's been about you."

EIGHTEEN

Vaughn

"Oh, God, I'm nervous," Vale murmurs from the passenger seat.

Our fingers are threaded together as I drive the two of us to Aiden's. I give her a reassuring squeeze. "I'm sure Aiden's worrying enough for the three of us. It'll be fine."

She bites on her bottom lip and nods. After a moment, she lets out a ragged breath. "Are we okay?"

"The three of us?"

"Yeah."

"It's not just about sex," I remind her. "Just like we told him at dinner last night."

She nods rapidly. "I know. I just worry that without the sex, we're boring."

I snort as I turn into his neighborhood. Expensive

houses way out of my pay grade line the streets. "We watched a movie. Aiden ate popcorn off your tits. I hardly call that boring."

She grins at the memory but continues to fidget in her seat. "But we didn't have sex. At the coffee shop, before his dad came, we were planning…" She huffs. "Sex."

"Aiden just likes being with us," I assure her. "With or without my impressive dick entering the scene."

"Ha," she deadpans.

"You're cute when you're sassy," I tell her with a smile.

Her features soften as I pull into the driveway where the GPS has sent us. "Vaughn?"

"Yeah, baby?"

"We haven't fought in weeks."

Since Aiden joined us officially.

"We may have been broken, but we weren't un-fixable," I tell her firmly. "We just needed some glue."

We climb out of the car and Aiden is already coming out the front door. After the movie last night, Aiden went home to smooth things over with his dad. He later texted us to tell us dinner was still on and his dad wasn't being so unreasonable about it all. This evening, he seems excited.

He reaches Vale first and he picks her up, spinning her. She squeals with laughter, making my heart clench in my chest. When he finally releases her, he walks over to me and boldly kisses me on the lips.

"Where's my kiss?" she says, pouting.

He grips her jaw with his palm and kisses her hard until her knees are wobbling. I laugh and pop her ass as I pass them. "No jealousy, woman. Rule number one."

They both chuckle from behind me.

"Come on," Aiden says, passing by me with Vale's hand in his. "My brother and his fiancée are already here. Ava and I almost have dinner ready."

When we walk into his massive house, a twinge of regret slices through me. I chose the education field knowing it wasn't the highest paying career. Normally, I don't mind. Times like these remind me of what I don't have. Aiden, though, doesn't seem like I'm a step down from his cushy life as he saunters through his house to find his family.

"Your house is so nice," Vale praises as she admires the décor.

"It didn't use to be this nice. Dad was a shitty decorator, but Ava eventually put her touch on everything."

"I heard that," Quinn grumbles from the dining

room as we start to pass through.

Aiden laughs and playfully punches his dad, who seems a lot more relaxed than yesterday. I walk over to him and offer my hand.

"Vaughn Young. We weren't properly introduced before."

He shakes my hand, firm and fierce. I'd expect nothing less of a man of his caliber. "Quinn Blakely."

"We're going to go check on Ava and Steph," Aiden says to me, leaving me alone with his father. I try not to cringe.

"Sure," I say and smile his way.

When I turn to regard Quinn, he's watching me warily. Fuck, this man doesn't trust easily.

"Aiden says you're his professor," he says bluntly.

At least I know where Aiden gets his no-non-sense personality. Always gets straight to the point. Difference with Aiden and Quinn is that Aiden de-livers it in a softer manner. Quinn is all edges and scowls.

"I am. I teach both macro and microeconomics."

He nods and walks over to a cabinet that hous-es liquor. I'm thankful to have something to take the edge off. He pours some brandy into two tumblers and hands me one.

"Aiden is a good kid," he says.

"A good man," I correct.

A frown wrinkle forms between his brows. "Don't remind me I'm getting old."

I chuckle. "Just telling it like it is."

He lets out a heavy sigh before sipping from his drink. "He and I had a long talk last night. He told me about your problems."

Shame courses through me. Each day that passes, I realize more and more that I was so weak to let my marriage nearly fall apart.

"Everyone has problems," he says. "My first wife and I couldn't get past ours. Had fifteen years of marriage not drained away, I would've never found Ava."

I nod, refusing to interrupt him when he doesn't, at present, look like he wants to kick my ass.

"Did Aiden tell you how we met?"

I arch a brow. "No, but something tells me it's a good story considering she's not much older than your sons, right?"

He laughs and right then he looks just like Aiden. "She was their babysitter. Barely legal. She had me all kinds of fucked in the head."

I smirk at him. "But she was the one."

"She was the one," he repeats, smiling fondly.

"You know of that. You found the one."

My smile fades. "I did. She's still the one. But we..." I drain my glass and set it down on the table. "We were on the brink of divorce."

"Divorce?"

"My buddy Dane drew up the papers and everything."

He grins. "You know Dane Alexander?"

"Who doesn't know Dane Alexander?" I joke. "He's a good guy. Known him for years. Asshole tried to talk me out of getting a divorce. What kind of divorce lawyer does that?"

He chuckles. "A shitty one."

"It was your son who made me tear the papers up," I admit. "He was so adamant about us staying together. He didn't want us to break apart, certainly not over him."

Quinn scowls, but pride flickers in his eyes. "He has a good head on his shoulders."

He pours us both more to drink. I can hear laughter and babies squealing from the kitchen. I think it's safe to say everything is going okay in there. I'm the one charged with calming the beast of the house.

"We tried. For a while there, before I took the step to have Dane draw up divorce papers, we took

Aiden's advice and tried to work on our marriage. But we were too far gone," I say sadly. I sip the brandy and let out a sigh. "We slipped back into old routines."

"And my son helped you find your way again?"

"Yeah. We feel stronger than ever. But truth is, if he were to walk away right now, I'd be plagued with worry that we wouldn't last without him." I frown at my admission. "Sorry, man, didn't mean to unload."

"So he's just something to hold you together."

I lift my gaze from my tumbler to stare him right in his eyes. "He's not something to us. He's everything."

When we're all seated around the table, I take a moment to look at Aiden's twin. To me they look exactly the same and nothing alike. It's their mannerisms that make them different. Now that I've met Anthony, I can tell he's the one who's the most like their father. He has his father's suspicious glare down pat. His fiancée, on the other hand, is bubbly and always smiling. Sometimes when he's simply glaring at me, she swats at him, whispers something in his ear, and has him grinning in a way that makes him look exactly like his handsome twin.

The real gem at the table, though, is Ava. She's quirky and a little on the nerdy side, but it's fascinating to watch the big, growly Quinn Blakely submit to her every whim. His eyes only ever leave hers to check on their adorable toddlers. I've seen the same intensity in Aiden's gaze before, which has a thrill shooting through me. I knew Aiden was into this polyamorous relationship with us, but verifying it by seeing it in another viewpoint with how his father regards his stepmother is a whole new perspective I can appreciate.

And Vale?

She's died and gone to baby heaven. The baby, June, sits on my wife's lap and tugs at her chunky necklaces as she tries to eat them. Vale has kissed that baby's head no less than fifty times since dinner started. I don't think she's even touched her food.

Guilt niggles at me.

I'll never be able to give her this.

As if in tune with my sudden mood change, Aiden leans in. "You okay?"

"Of course," I say lightly, despite the gruffness hiding in my tone.

He pats my thigh and then starts talking to his brother about website design. I tune them out to watch Vale. Her smile is bright but fake. To all these people, she's happy. But I've seen the defeated look in her pretty green eyes before. Something she wants so badly is the very thing she cannot have. It nearly destroyed us.

Fuck, if I could give her a baby, I would've done it eight years ago.

When Vale's gaze falls to June's head and she doesn't look up again, I know she's fighting tears. Since we've all finished up, I figure we should leave.

"I think we're going to head out," I say to everyone. "She won't admit it, but my wife has a migraine."

She shoots me a thankful look. "I'll be fine," she says lamely. "Besides, we can't leave them with this mess."

Stephanie, Anthony's fiancée, scoffs. "Nonsense, honey. Get out of here and take care of that migraine. We'll put Anthony on dishes. Right, baby?"

He rolls his eyes but pulls her hand to him so he can kiss her knuckle over her engagement ring. "If that makes you happy, teacup."

She beams at him. "It's settled then. You guys go home. It was wonderful finally meeting you all."

Everyone says their goodbyes and Aiden follows us out. Vale gets inside the car while Aiden and I stare after her.

"She okay?"

I let out a sigh. "Nope."

"I'm coming over. Let me grab a bag." He gives my shoulder a squeeze and runs back inside.

A huge weight lifts from my shoulders. Normally, I try to pull her out of these dark moments on my own and almost always I fuck it up. But Aiden? He's a natural. I'm thankful as hell he's coming with us. In less than five minutes he trots back out and takes my keys.

"I'm driving," he says with an easy grin.

He's been driving this relationship since the moment we opened the door to our marriage and let him in. "Thank you."

His eyes meet mine and understanding dawns in his eyes.

I'll never be able to thank him enough for how he's able to reach inside her and distract her from what we'll never have.

Chapter

NINETEEN

Vale

T hey're tag teaming me.

Emotion clogs my throat as I excuse myself to the bathroom once we're home. I can hear them chatting in low voices in the bedroom while I hide out from them. When I think about Aiden's little sister June and her twin brothers Jayden and Joseph, a deep, heavy ache settles in the pit of my belly.

Envy.

I'm envious of Quinn's cute little wife, Ava, and her ability to pop out children left and right. I just want one. I want one baby to hold and call mine. I'm not that greedy. Vaughn says we can adopt—that he'd love to if that'd make me happy—but I've never pulled the trigger on that decision. It makes me a horrible person, but I don't want to adopt. It's more heartache and waiting and stress. There is no easy answer.

I sit on the edge of the bathtub as tears roll down my cheeks. Now that the dam has been broken, they won't stop. Shame fills me for so many reasons. Aiden will get to see the real me. The me who obsesses over what she can't have. The me who destroys her own relationships because of one thing that consumes her so fully.

I'll push him away too.

It's what I do.

"You okay in there, beautiful?" Aiden asks from the door.

I choke on a sob. "Yep."

"Big fat liar."

A laugh escapes me through my tears.

"Open the door, Vale."

"In a minute," I utter.

"Now."

"I'm pooping."

He snorts. "You're not pooping. Let me in."

There's no hiding. I'm sure Vaughn filled him in on every gory detail of what a terribly obsessed person I am over infertility. I just can't let go of it. No matter how hard I try.

"Now."

I let out an exasperated sigh and stand. I turn the lock and start to back away, but he swings the door open, prowling over to me. I expect Vaughn to join the party, but he doesn't come inside. I'm thankful not to have them both glaring down at me.

"You're so pretty when you cry," he murmurs, swiping his thumb across my cheek. "But I don't like it. I prefer your smiles, beautiful."

A smile breaches my face. "You're distracting."

"Come here and let me distract you some more."

His palms find my ass and he pulls me to him. I let out a sigh as he kisses me gently. Then, he rests his forehead on mine. "It's okay to be sad. It's a sad thing."

Tears well in my eyes again as I nod. "I'm sorry."

He scowls. "What in the hell would you ever have to be sorry for?"

"It won't go away," I choke out. "Something like this doesn't just go away. That sense of failure follows me around like a fog." More tears leak out and his eyes track them down my cheeks.

"Baby," he says softly. "Our pain is what defines us. I'm not sure you'd be the deep, emotional, vulnerable soul you are without it. I like all the parts of you. Even those jagged not-so-pretty ones."

"You do?"

He nods. "And guess what?"

"What?"

"He does too."

The he in question appears in the doorway. Concern is written all over his features. I do what I should have done over and over again all these years. I go to him and let him hold me. Vaughn is stiff at first, but then he squeezes me tight.

He never wanted to fix me. He just wanted to hold all the broken parts of me so I wouldn't lose myself.

When I feel Aiden's heat behind me as he sandwiches me between them, I relax. The hurt and heartache melts away as I let these two men keep me together. We remain locked in this position for a long time. The only thing that can be heard is our rhythmic breathing and the clock ticking on the bathroom wall.

At some point, the bathroom becomes warm. I tilt my head up and meet the loving stare of my husband. His fingers thread into my hair and he kisses me deeply. Apologies and heartache and hope all rolled into one kiss. I cling to him desperately. Behind me, Aiden slides my hair to the side and starts to kiss the side of my neck. I let out a breathy mewl that has both men hardening against me.

Vaughn breaks away but clutches onto my hands as he walks us backward into the bedroom. When he reaches the bed, he unbuttons his shirt and sheds it. As he undresses, Aiden holds me to him. The moment Vaughn is fully naked, he steps forward and starts removing my clothes. Behind me, I can hear Aiden getting undressed as well.

"Lie down," Vaughn instructs. "We want to take care of you."

I bite down on my bottom lip and search both their expressions. No resentment or annoyance. The same heated, protective look shines in both their eyes. Obeying my husband, I sit down on the bed and lie back.

"Spread your legs so we can see your perfect pussy, Vale," Vaughn murmurs.

A cool draft of air hits the part of me that aches with need. Aiden's eyes become wolfish as he follows Vaughn's stare to my pussy.

"We never got dessert," Aiden muses aloud, his lips quirking up on one side. "I'm hungry. How about you?"

Vaughn's grin is nearly evil. "I was craving something sweet. Want to share?"

Both my evil boys smile down at me as they stare

at me like I'm the finest meal they'll ever have. A shiver of part desire, part apprehension shudders down me. As much as we've fucked and messed around, they haven't done this together. I'm curious as to how it will go down.

Vaughn kneels and Aiden mimics his action. They each grab one of my knees and spread me farther apart. I sit up on my elbows so I can watch them. Vaughn kisses my clit and then Aiden leans in to run his tongue along my slit. I let out a gasp.

Vaughn winks at me but instead of diving back in, he turns to kiss Aiden. Their kiss is ravenous as they devour the other. It turns me on and I can't help but reach between my thighs to relieve some of the ache that throbs to my core. Aiden pushes my hand away, causing me to grumble. Both men chuckle as they break their kiss. Aiden starts kissing along my inner thigh where Vaughn has taken to nipping my flesh with his teeth on the other side. They're teasing me everywhere except the place that practically drips in desperation for them.

Aiden climbs onto the bed as Vaughn settles on the floor between my thighs. They kiss again, right over my pussy, but before I complain, they start kissing me there. I let out a loud gasp of air when their tongues fight to tease my clit. Two tongues swirling and lashing at my most sensitive place at once has me squirming on the bed. Since Aiden's on the bed with me, he uses his strong arm to pin my lower half to keep me from moving.

"She's so sweet," Aiden praises, his hot breath sending my senses haywire.

"So sweet," Vaughn agrees.

Then I feel someone's teeth. Oh God. Aiden's tongue wins the battle for my clit as Vaughn seeks out other areas to pleasure me. When his tongue pushes against my entrance, I let out a moan.

"This feels so good," I croak out. I grab at my tits, desperate to take out my ecstasy on something.

Aiden sucks on my clit as Vaugh starts fucking my hole with his tongue. It's too much. Too intense. They're going to drive me crazy. It doesn't take long until I'm screaming and thrashing in pleasure. They assault my senses until tears are leaking from my eyes. Too much pleasure. Too intense.

"Oh my God," I rasp out when they finally pull away. "That was amazing."

"About damn time," Aiden says, laughing. "I knew I was better than good at something."

Vaughn chuckles as he stands. He affectionately

squeezes Aiden's shoulder before pointing to the bed. "Vale," my husband says, gaining my attention. "I want you to ride this good-looking man's cock."

We shuffle around and before I slide over Aiden's cock, I look at Vaughn. He lifts a brow and follows my gaze to the open drawer. His hand reaches in but instead of grabbing the condoms, he grabs the lube. My eyes dart to his. He gives me a small nod of his approval. When I look down at Aiden, he's smiling at me.

"I'm clean," he assures me. "When I found out my last girlfriend was fucking around on me, I went ahead and got myself checked out."

"I'm not on the pill," I remind him. Not that I can get pregnant anyway.

"We're not going to hope or dream for something we can't control," Aiden murmurs, his palm sliding around the back of my neck. He pulls me close until our lips are nearly touching. "No more obsessing. You'll let us distract you, right?"

Our lips fuse together as I rub against his naked cock.

"Words, Vale. I need your promise."

"I promise."

He grabs my hips and I easily slide down his length. It feels so much better without a condom.

"Attention here," Aiden growls. "I need your eyes and complete focus. I'm going to have to talk you through this."

Panic makes me shudder as the bed dips behind me. The popping of the cap of the lube bottle has me jolting.

"Baby," Vaughn murmurs as he gives my ass an affectionate squeeze. "I would never hurt you. You tell us to stop and that's the end."

"Okay," I breathe. "I want to try this."

For weeks now, they've taken turns fingering me with three and four fingers. Stretching me. Readying me for this moment. But I'm nervous. Vaughn's tongue was just inside me and that felt like a stretch. The vagina is a fascinating part of human anatomy that it can grow to accommodate up to ten centimeters. It's by some divine design that it can shrink back to its original size.

At least that's what I keep telling myself.

"What if it doesn't go back?" I say in a moment of panic.

Both of the men caress me, but it's Aiden who assures me.

"I've done this before. Trust me, baby, it goes back."

His mouth attacks mine and I let him kiss me dizzy. Vaughn rubs his slippery dick along my ass crack but that's not where he's going.

"Relax," Aiden says against my mouth. "Let him in."

I nod and Vaughn gives me another loving squeeze on my ass. When I feel Vaughn's fingers slip inside me beside Aiden's dick, I let out a moan. His fingers tease me as Aiden remains absolutely still. As soon as my husband removes his fingers, I feel a loss.

I want this.

I want them both.

"We're doing this," Vaughn rasps out as the crown of his cock tries to find a point of entry beside Aiden's massive cock.

I kiss Aiden to distract myself from the fear of something bad happening. But Vaughn is slowly easing in and caressing my ass in a reverent way. Aiden grips my hair and looks intently in my eyes.

"Let him in," he urges.

Vaughn grunts from behind me. The stretching burns, but it's not awful. I dig my nails into Aiden's shoulders.

"Vaughn," he barks out in warning.

Vaughn pauses. "Am I hurting you?"

"N-No," I breathe. "I'm just nervous."

They both wait me out. So patient and loving.

"Do it," I whisper.

I can feel Vaughn's hand on his dick brushing against me as he holds it steady while pushing inside me. Once his crown breaches my opening, his lubed cock slides easily in.

Holy shit.

I've never felt so…full.

"Talk to me, Vale," Aiden orders, his brows furling together in concern. But his lips are parted. This feels good for him.

Slowly, I push back against them, forcing Vaughn deeper. Both men hiss in pleasure. The choked sounds escaping them and the fact I'm not ripping apart gives me more confidence.

"Fuck me," I plead. "I want to feel like you both want this as much as I do."

Both men let out similar growls as both their hips flex at once. I'm impaled deeper by two thick cocks. I cry out in pleasure. It's a burning, exciting type of feeling. Different than what I'm used to.

"Touch her clit," Vaughn orders to Aiden.

As soon as Aiden works his hand between us, I start to lose my mind. Now that coupled with the way they stretch me out has pleasure surging through me. But when Vaughn rubs a slippery thumb against my asshole, I know I'm about to be sent hurtling into some new realm. The burn of his thumb breaching my ass does send me over the edge. I black out in pleasure as my climax rips through me and I cry out. My entire body trembles uncontrollably.

"Fuck her good," Aiden barks out. "Fuck her hard."

He's a little trapped beneath us so his movements are limited. He makes up for it by rubbing my clit so hard he sends me into another orgasm. I'm slick with sweat between them and am at their glorious mercy. They continue fucking me until they quickly unravel. Heat floods inside of me and I know it's Vaughn who's come first based on the way he groans. His cum works as a fresh lubricant that has us really slipping and sliding. Aiden lets out a choked growl as he comes too.

"Oh, God," I whimper. "That was…wild."

Aiden laughs as Vaughn slowly eases out of me. Aiden's cock, now soft, slides out of me when he rolls me to my back. Vaughn sidles up on my other side and he smiles happily down at me.

"I can settle for wild," Aiden says with an easy smile. "As long as you're happy."

Tears well in my eyes because I'm overwhelmed by emotion. When Vaughn frowns with worry, I stroke his stubbly cheek.

"I'm very happy," I tell them both. "I haven't been this happy in a long time."

Chapter

TWENTY

Aiden

Two months later…

"This is the smartest thing we've done yet," Vale says with pride as she admires her busy coffee shop.

Wi-Fi.

Free Wi-Fi.

I chuckle as I ring up a customer and then steal a kiss from her. The shop is bustling. People don't just run in for coffee and go. Now, we rival some of the chain coffee shops with our lingering college students and business people. Some will stay for hours at the same table working on projects. It looks good for potential customers too to see it so busy. This was the first month Vale wasn't in the red.

"I still think the smartest thing was taking down

those hideous curtains," I tease.

She swats at me. "Asshole."

Another customer comes in and while she takes care of them, I grab a wet rag and the disinfectant to clean off some tables. I love this place. Since I've had such a hand in making it better, I feel a sense of pride. Even Dad and Anthony drop by to throw in their two cents on how to bring in more clientele, which makes me happy to know they care.

Vale laughs at her customer and I stare at her. All she does is smile and giggle. Such a far cry from the woman I met months ago. Back when her marriage was on the rocks. Her marriage is solid now. I love feeling like I have been instrumental in keeping it together.

Some days, I wonder about the future. I let it eat at me some, but Vale and Vaughn are both intuitive. When I feel worried, they distract me. Just like when Vale got upset after meeting my siblings for the first time, we came together to distract her.

My phone buzzes in my pocket and I grin to see it's Vaughn.

Vaughn: I got us tickets to see a movie later.

Me: Which movie?

Vaughn: I'll give you three guesses and the first

two don't count.

I snort because I know.

Me: Let me guess. Dwayne Johnson's newest one.
Vaughn: Vale's favorite.

She's seen all of his movies probably a hundred times each. It's cute. We like to give her shit about her crush, although she says she likes him for his acting ability.

"Aiden?"

My smile falls when I see Alani Rice staring at me. I'm immediately tense at seeing her. Last year, we fucked around and dated. I lost my virginity to her and then had sex with her cousin Jaime. It was where I really explored whether or not I liked males or females. I'd loved everything about pussy and Alani's cute tits, but all it took was her cousin Jaime to pull his dick out and then I was all over him too. Eventually, Jaime got bored and I stayed with Alani. That is, until she cheated on me.

"You look good," she says. "Still working at a bakery, I see."

Her gaze falls to my wrist. Last summer her fucking dad broke my arm when I pretended to be my brother.

"Yep," I grunt.

She bites on her bottom lip in a way I used to find irresistible. Not anymore. I want her to leave.

"I'm enjoying college," she says lightly.

I force a smile. "Me too. I stayed local."

"So I heard."

She lets out a heavy sigh. "I'm in for the weekend visiting Dad, but maybe we could have dinner or something. I feel really bad about how we ended things."

"I'm in a relationship," I tell her, my eyes drifting to Vale.

Vale flashes me a sweet smile before turning back to her customer. She reaches to take their money and her wedding ring glimmers under the light.

"That's her?" Alani asks. "A married woman?"

I jerk my gaze back her way. "It's none of your business."

Her lips purse together. "The husband too?"

I hate that she knows me so well. "You should go."

"Oh," she mutters. "I wasn't trying to offend you. I just…" She trails off and frowns. "You of all people know it's too hard when three people try to make it work."

"It's hard for anything to work when one of the people is out spreading her legs for the whole football team," I bite out.

She blinks at me in shock. I've always been one to play nicely, but right now I'm feeling anything but. I don't like that I feel the need to defend my relationship to Alani of all people.

"You should go," I say softer. "I'm glad you're doing well."

Her smile is fake as she walks away. I walk over to Vale and give her a hug, taking strength from her warm embrace.

"Everything okay?" she asks.

"It is now."

I'm tense as we head into the movie theater. Vaughn has his fingers threaded with Vale's as they absently stare at up-and-coming movie posters on the walls. For a spilt, bitter second, I feel like an outsider. It's stupid because before Alani showed up this afternoon, I'd been completely content.

But she planted a seed of doubt inside me.

Hell, maybe the seed was already there and she just watered it.

Regardless, I'm beginning to wonder just how

well this relationship will work. When it's three different people with no prior life tying them together, everyone feels on equal ground. But Vale and Vaughn love each other. I'm going into it with an unfair advantage.

Vale clutches my bicep. "You okay?"

I give her a clipped nod and walk up to the concessions counter. We tell the woman our order and then I toss some twenties on the glass to pay. Vaughn shoots me a questioning glare and I shrug my shoulders at him.

"Why the sudden attitude?" Vaughn demands, slinging his arm over my shoulders.

He hands the man our tickets and we walk past him. I feel like everyone is eyeing us. Are we freaks now? Did I make them freaks? I clench my jaw and shake him off me, nearly dropping my drink in the process. I can hear them whispering to each other behind me as we walk into the theater. When we reach the top, Vaughn points at a seat. I drop into it and place my drink in the holder. They take a seat on either side of me, boxing me in. Normally, I'd be super fucking happy about that, but right now, I don't know how I feel.

Annoyed.

Frustrated.

Confused.

Vale tries to take my hand, but I start opening my box of candy, ignoring her. She settles her palm on my thigh and pats me. My chest aches because I know my sudden moodiness is confusing her. Probably hurting her feelings.

But Vaughn?

He's pissed.

I can feel his stare burning into me as the previews start. I try to tune them both out as I attempt to work out how my future with them plays out.

They'll find their way back to each other and push me out.

Bitterness tightens its hold around my heart.

What they have for each other is love. What they have for me is lust. As much as I care for them, I'm nothing but a device in their marriage. Something to rekindle what they've lost. Pain aches in my chest. My brother always tells me I feel too much. That I dive into every relationship head first. I wish I could change that about myself, but I can't. Especially not now. With Vale and Vaughn, I put every ounce of me into this thing we're doing.

But what happens at the end?

When the fucking credits are rolling?

They'll leave hand in hand, and I'll trail behind them. Bitter and lost.

A strong hand curls behind my neck and pulls me to him. Vaughn's hot breath is in my ear the next instant. "Whatever's going on in your head, we're going to talk about it tonight."

"I'm not staying over tonight," I grit out.

"The hell you're not," he grumbles. "You're coming home with us and you're going to tell me what the hell has you so upset." He squeezes the back of my neck in an affectionate way. "So we can fix it."

I swallow down the emotion and stare blindly at the screen. He's waiting for a reaction, so I give him a simple nod. Eventually he releases me to take my hand. Vale pulls my box of candy away and then her hand takes my other. I close my eyes, trying desperately to push the self-doubt away and enjoy this with them. I hate that one meeting with Alani and I'm second-guessing everything.

Vale rubs comforting circles on my hand with her thumb while Vaughn squeezes me so tight, I think he'll crush the bones in my hand. They don't seem like two people ready to let me go. The thought of them sitting across from me, as a united front, telling me we're done, has the candy souring in my stomach.

She leans over the armrest and props her head on my shoulder. My heart feels like it's cracking down the middle. When I broke up with people in my past relationships, it stung. But if it happens with these two, I know it's going to hurt a lot worse. I'm too attached. I fucking warned them I would be.

I watch the rest of the movie in a daze.

I should break it off with them. Move on before I make an even bigger mess of their lives. My heart sinks.

I couldn't do that if I tried.

It won't be me breaking up with them, that's for sure.

Which means when they finally let me go, it'll be my heart that gets crushed in the process, and there'll be no way of stopping it.

"I think I'm going to head out," I tell them, standing awkwardly in their kitchen.

Vale frowns and shakes her head. "No."

I lift my brows and scoff. "Okayyyy."

"You're not going anywhere," Vaughn grumbles.

"You're going to get your ass upstairs and in that bed where you belong."

"Because I'm your fuck toy," I snap. "Got it. Almost forgot my place in this game."

Vaughn's jaw clenches and Vale gasps.

"Aiden," she whispers. "You're not…"

"This isn't a fucking game," Vaughn growls, prowling my way. "It's our fucking life." He points at her and then himself before poking my chest. "*Our* life."

He leans his forehead against mine and some of the tension bleeds from me. When Vale hugs me from behind, I find myself relaxing against Vaughn. He's coiled tight, but he wraps an arm around me, hugging me to him.

"Don't self-sabotage," he rumbles. "Because you're not the only person who gets hurt."

Guilt slices through me. "I'm sorry," I choke out. "I just don't know how to navigate this shit."

Vale sniffles and more guilt assaults me. "We navigate it together," she tells me, her voice shaking with emotion. "Please don't distance yourself from us."

I turn my head and Vaughn does the same. His lips meet mine as he kisses me in a desperate way I've yet to experience from him. Like he's scared. Like he almost lost me and he can't believe I'm still here. The thought has my heart kick-starting to life. I break from his kiss and pull away to turn toward Vale. Tears streak down her pretty red cheeks and I palm her face, swiping the wetness away with my thumbs. "I'm sorry," I tell her. "I just freaked the fuck out for a bit there."

She smiles at me. "No more freaking out." I allow her to guide me out of the kitchen and upstairs while we leave Vaughn to close up the house for the night. Once in their bedroom, she starts pulling away my hoodie and shirt. When I'm just in my jeans, she yanks off her sweater, baring her cute tits that are barely concealed in her bra to me. My mouth waters to lick the valley between her breasts. Vaughn enters the room, his stare becoming wolfish as he takes in our half-naked bodies. He yanks off his own shirt and strides over to us.

"You're hot when you're pouty," Vaughn teases as his warm body presses against mine from behind. His large palms splay over my abs. "God, I love your stomach."

I chuckle when Vale nods in agreement.

All humor fades, though, when Vale removes the rest of her clothing. My eyes track her naked body as she rummages in the end table. She tosses a bottle of lube on the bed beside us before approaching me with hungry eyes.

"Take his pants off," she orders her husband. "We have to convince him to stay."

Heat burns through me when he starts deftly undoing my jeans. I let out a groan when his palm rubs over my hard dick over my boxers.

"Like this, baby?" he asks her as he strokes me.

She taps her bottom lip as though she's thinking. "He still has that panicked look in his eyes like he might run at any second. Pull his cock out, honey."

I can feel Vaughn smile against the side of my neck before he nips my skin there. "Of course, sweetheart."

She beams at us as he pulls my dick into his hand. His own erection is hard as fuck pressed against my ass.

"Maybe you should suck his nice cock," Vaughn suggests, his breath hot against my neck. "You suck cock so well, beautiful. I'm sure you could convince him better than I could."

She steps closer and wraps her hand over his so they stroke me together. I let out a hiss of pleasure.

"I don't know," she says, batting her lashes. "I've

seen the way you suck his cock, Vaughn, and I have to say, he really likes it."

He pushes my boxers down my thighs and then he works on his own pants. Soon, his naked dick is rubbing against the crack of my ass.

"I know of other ways to make him feel good," Vaughn growls. "Get on your knees, baby. It's important you do it really fucking well. We want to keep him. Make him want to stay."

She drops to her knees and her plump lips wrap around my dick. Hot and wet. Feels fucking wonderful. I run my fingers through her silky hair and grip her tight. She allows me to take over the pace as I slowly fuck her face.

"Now that's an image that gets me really fucking hard," Vaughn rumbles as he reaches for the lube. "But I'm too greedy to sit back and watch. No, I want to have a hand in making you want to stay."

He squirts the lube on his dick and then he slides it against my crack.

"Put your palms on the bed," he orders to me. And then to Vale, "Keep sucking, baby."

We shuffle until my legs are parted with Vale beneath me. Slowly, I rock my hips, fucking her pretty mouth. Vaughn's strong grip holds me in place as the tip of his fat cock presses against my asshole.

"You're not going anywhere," Vaughn hisses as his dick slides inside of me, stretching me with his thickness. "You're staying right here where we can enjoy you." He thrusts hard and Vale gags. "And not just for sex, goddammit. We like taking you to the fucking movies and dinner."

She pops off, licks the tip of my dick, and then looks up at me. "We do. I love working with you. You make me laugh."

Vaughn thrusts hard again, making me groan in pleasure. "And I like fucking looking at you. Even when you're pouting and feeling sorry for yourself." His palm comes around to stroke my cock and then he grips Vale's hair, pulling her closer. "Mouth on his cock, baby."

When her lips slide back over my length, my knees nearly buckle. They're driving me crazy in a good way. I certainly don't feel like a fuck toy. I feel wanted and adored.

Vaughn pulls nearly all the way out of my ass, the crown of his dick stretching my opening, before he slides back in. "Feel the way I own your ass?" he growls in question.

"Fuck yes," I grunt.

"And feel the way my wife's throat chokes your dick?"

She hums in agreement, making me dizzy with pleasure.

"No one," he rumbles. "No one outside of this bedroom can make you feel the way we do."

He starts fucking me harder and Vale enthusiastically sucks on my dick. We get caught up in the moment. No more talking. Just grunts and moans. Murmurs of praise. Our bodies making sloppy sounds that are fucking hot as hell.

And then I'm coming.

I start to pull out, but Vale tightens her grip on my thighs, deep throating me. I drain my release down her throat as Vaughn pulls out of me suddenly. Heat spurts against my ass as he comes. I wish I could see his face right now. Fuck, these two people are going to kill me.

With a grunt, I pull out of her mouth and admire her. Slobber runs down her chin and her hair is a wild mess. Her green eyes glimmer with appreciation for me and pride that she could bring me to orgasm. I caress her cheek lovingly.

"Thank you."

She rises and kisses me. "You're welcome. Now

hurry and recover because it's my turn to get fucked."

I look over my shoulder at Vaughn and he laughs. "You're young," he says with a wickedly delicious glint in his eyes. "You'll be hard and ready to fuck long before I am. I'm going to grab a shower. I'd like to hear her screams as I wash my dick."

We laugh at him as he saunters off, his muscled ass flexing. My dick flinches back to life. I wrap my arms around her and lay us down on the bed. We kiss and tease while the shower runs. My fingers slide between her thighs where I find her dripping with arousal. With my tongue dancing with hers, I rub against her clit until she's clawing at me, screaming out her orgasm.

Vaughn hoots from the shower, making us both laugh. Then, we grow serious when I spread her thighs apart and sink deep inside her tight cunt.

"God, you feel amazing," I whisper, peppering kisses all over her pretty face.

"You feel pretty awesome yourself." She grins at me, her lashes fluttering.

"Awesome, huh?"

"Sooo awesome."

I thrust into her slowly and our smiles fade. Our eyes remain locked as I make love to her. It's not frantic or rushed. Reverently, I run my palm over her tit and squeeze it. She closes her eyes and the walls of her pussy clench. I let out a groan and kiss her mouth. Her fingers stroke through my hair and I devour all her sweet sighs. When her soft breaths become loud moans, I fuck her a little harder.

The bed sinks down beside us and I lock eyes with Vaughn's burning stare as he lies on his side, watching us. He fists his cock as he watches me fuck her. She and I both turn to watch the way he jerks at his dick. They kiss and it sends me over the edge. My hips piston into her wildly until I'm coming. I don't hear her coming yet, so I furiously rub at her clit until she cries out, clamping hard around my dick. Vaughn's breath hitches and then he groans. His cum jets out and shoots against our sides.

"Fuck," I grunt as I fall against Vale's tits. I bury my face in her hair and inhale her. "Your pussy is so perfect."

She giggles and I can feel my cum run out of her from the movement. Sliding out of her, I sit up on my knees. Vaughn hands me his still wet towel. I clean her up and then my dick before settling between them on the bed. Vaughn's hard body curls around mine from behind as I pull Vale's curvy, soft one to me. I love the way they sandwich me in. Like I fit right here. Like I'm supposed to between them.

This feels right.

"You know where you belong," Vaughn murmurs, his voice husky.

"With us," Vale says.

I close my eyes and allow my body to finally relax. "This feels right."

"It *is* right," the both say at once.

It is right.

Chapter

TWENTY-ONE

Aiden

Three months later…

I'm too tired to pay attention to Easton's sermon and I find my mind drifting to Vale and Vaughn. I'd invited them to church with me today since Stephanie begged me to go, but Vaughn had some papers to grade and Vale wasn't feeling well. I left them with the promise I'd bring her back some chicken noodle soup and that I'd help him when I returned.

My heart warms at thinking about the past few months. I'd hit a hiccup in our relationship when I'd nearly let my self-doubt destroy us. But they convinced me to stay and I haven't looked back since.

I stifle a yawn and Stephanie swats at me. I shrug and bite back a smile. Anthony snorts at us, earning annoyed stares from others in the congregation. He and I will catch hell for this after church. My brother winks at me. I think he likes getting in trouble with his woman.

Easton prattles on and eventually the service is over. While people are hugging and chatting, I slip out of the church and step into the hallway. I pull out my phone and text Vale.

Me: Chicken noodle soup or broccoli cheddar? Ask Vaughn if he wants anything. I'm about to leave here.

Her response is immediate.

Vale: We need to talk. Come home right after.

Unease slithers down my spine. She'd seemed off this morning. Sort of grumpy, but I'd chalked it up to being sick.

Me: Sure, babe.

When she doesn't respond, my nerves eat me alive. I text Vaughn instead.

Me: Everything okay?

The dots move and then stop. Move and then stop.

Vaughn: Are you on your way here?

I scrub my palm down over my face. When Easton steps into the hallway and sees me, his brows furl and he excuses himself from whomever he was speaking to.

"Hey, Aiden, want to meet me in my office?" he asks, concern in his voice.

Nodding, I follow after him and am thankful when the door closes behind him.

"You doing all right, man?" he asks.

I swallow and shoot him a panicked look. "I hope so."

"What's going on?" he demands. "You look like you're going to be sick."

Maybe I've caught Vale's illness. My hand shakes and I fist it. "I don't feel so good."

"Sit down," he instructs. Instead of taking his desk chair, he sits beside me in the pair in front of his desk. "How's the relationship going?"

He got to meet them both last month over dinner at Steph's house. Everyone got along great, much to my surprise. I'd expected Easton to be judgmental, but I should have known better. He's a good friend and took it all in stride. Vale and Lacy connected really well. They whispered quietly in one corner of the room and by their teary eyes, I could tell they were sharing stories of pain. I was happy as hell she had someone who somehow knew what sort of pain she's been through.

"It was going great," I utter, my voice tight.

"Until…"

I hand him my phone. He reads through the recent texts. "I think you're worrying yourself sick over nothing," he says, setting my phone back in my palm.

I clench my jaw and nod. "Probably."

But what if I'm wrong? What if we're both wrong? What if the strange way she'd acted and then their odd texts means it's finally over.

I scrub my palm over my face, a shuddering breath tumbling out of me. "I love them."

He leans forward, resting his elbows on his knees, and regards me with a gentle expression. "I'm sure they love you too."

"And if they don't?"

He smiles. "You're too easy to love, kid. Hell, I even love you." He reaches forward and tries to ruffle my hair.

I crack a smile and swat him away. "I'm being serious."

"I know. A little too serious," he grunts. "I've seen the three of you together. At first, I was skeptical and a bit worried. But I saw the way their eyes lit up when you were close. I saw the way yours would track them from across the room. It's the same way I look at my wife and how she looks at me. Love, man. There is love between you all. It may not be normal or what is generally accepted, but it's there."

"Is God gonna strike me where I sit?"

He snorts. "I told you, knucklehead, God is all about the love. When it's good and selfless and pure, it's the right kind of love. Stop worrying your panties into a wad."

I laugh. "You're a bad preacher."

"Someone has to lead all the hooligans down the right path," he says, grinning. "You gotta be one helluva hooligan yourself to be able to do that."

Letting out a sigh, I rise to my feet. He does the same and I hug my buddy. "Fine, I guess you're okay."

He pats my back and releases me. "Now go settle your mind. Tell them how you feel if that is something you're holding back. Whatever it is, try not to let it eat you up."

I give him a nod. "What if they really want to break it off with me, though?"

His brows furl together. "Then we'll get through it together. I'm here to talk if you need me. I'm a phone call away."

"Thanks, man."

I pray to God he's right and that everything's

going to be okay.

It has to be.

I unlock the front door and step inside the house. There are some grocery bags sitting on the counter and the house smells as though they've just eaten. I frown as I hunt them down. When I round the corner into the living room, they both jerk their stares at me. Vale sits in Vaughn's lap in the recliner and they're holding hands. He's dressed, but she's still wearing a T-shirt and not much else.

"Hey," I grunt.

"How was church?" Vaughn asks.

"It was fine." My voice is tight with nerves.

"Sit down," Vale says, pointing to the couch.

The vibe in the air is one I don't recognize and I hate it instantly. I don't like the way my stomach bottoms out. This doesn't feel happy or good. It feels fucking stressful.

I shoot Vaughn a panicked look and his features are soft. "Sit."

Dropping to the middle cushion, I lean back and cross my arms over my chest. "What's up?" I say coolly, trying to hide the fact I'm about to freak the fuck out.

They both watch me, sadness flickering in their gazes. If they're so sad to get rid of me, then why are they? I can tell something pivotal is about to change and it fucking sucks.

"Listen," Vale starts, her voice trembling. "We have something to tell you."

"Just get it out already," I snap. "The suspense is fucking killing me."

Vale's bottom lip wobbles and she looks at Vaughn. His jaw clenches and he shoots me a glare.

"We need to talk about the dynamics of this relationship," Vaughn says. "The future."

Pain weighs heavily on me like a ton of bricks. I feel like my throat is closing up tight. Air is constricted and I can't fucking breathe. I lean forward and rest my elbows on my knees, palming my face in defeat. "A future that doesn't involve me," I whisper, my voice cracking with emotion. "Fuck."

I knew it was coming and I wanted to ignore it.

But how the hell can you ignore when your heart is being ripped from your chest?

When I feel the couch sink down on each side of me, my heart crushes a little more. I want nothing more than to pull them to me and not let go. I needed more warning than this. It's too sudden.

Vale's soft hand runs down my spine and Vaugh clutches my thigh.

"Please don't leave us," she begs tearfully.

I snap my head up and jerk my attention to her. She's crying now and I don't fucking get it.

"Me?" I hiss. "I don't want to leave."

Vaughn snorts. "You look like you're about to take off."

Turning, I regard him. His features are angry almost. "Because you're breaking it off with me."

"What?" Vale shrieks. "No!"

"Hell no," Vaughn growls.

"Then what the hell is up with all this future talk?" I demand.

Vaughn leans forward and presses his forehead to mine. His fingers run through my hair as he rumbles, "We love you, Aiden."

Relief floods through me and I angle my head up to kiss him. Then, I pull away to look at Vale.

"I love you guys too," I mutter.

She beams at me despite the tears rolling out. Her lips press to mine for a chaste kiss. "Good. I was hoping you'd say that."

"We want you to move in with us," Vaughn says, his voice gruff. "Permanently."

"That is, if you want to," Vale adds.

"Of course I want to," I blurt out. "I practically live here as it is."

"We're not done," Vaughn says softly. "There's more."

"I took a test this morning," Vale whispers, happiness shining in her eyes.

"A test?"

"She's going to have a baby," Vaughn explains, pride in his voice. "Our baby. A baby that was made out of love—love you brought back into this home."

I reach out and palm her stomach over her T-shirt. "Really? We're going to have a baby?"

She nods tearfully. "We are."

"And before you can start worrying your fucking head off, don't," Vaughn grunts. "We want you to stay and we want to do this together."

My mind is a mess of jumbled thoughts. "Who's the dad?"

Vale tenses. "My guess is you considering all the trouble we've had in the past. But it doesn't matter to us. Does it matter to you?"

Not really. I don't care if it's his or mine. It feels

like ours.

"I can be its dad?"

Vaughn grips my shoulder. "You are its dad."

"And so are you," Vale says to him. Then she regards me. "Is this okay? I feel like we're in strange waters, but I'm glad it's with you two. I feel like we can make it work. Together."

I lean back against the sofa and pull her into my lap. She stretches her legs across Vaughn's lap and curls against me.

"You two fucking scared me," I grumble. "I thought you were done with me."

Vale tilts her head up and kisses me. "We could never be done with you. You're the glue, Aiden. You hold the three of us together."

"Just how it should be," Vaughn adds, smiling.

"Then I'm in," I tell them, grinning. "I'm in it for the long haul."

Vaughn's smile turns wicked. "Not like you really had a choice. Our next plan was to lock you in the basement. Glad you chose to come willingly."

Smirking, I shrug. "Don't tease me with kinky shit."

Vale sits up and straddles my lap. "Oh? You want me to tie you up and have my dirty little way with you? I heard pregnancy hormones make a woman insatiable."

"It's a good thing our woman has two men to help take care of all her filthy needs," I say as I slide my palms to her ass.

Vaugh reaches over and caresses her tit through her shirt. "It sounds like you need your husband's fat dick in your ass while you fuck your baby daddy's thick cock to keep you satisfied."

Vale bites on her bottom lip and rocks her hips. "I think you two know me well."

A growl rumbles through Vaughn as I tear off her shirt in the same instant.

"No time like the present," I say to her before turning to Vaughn. "Let's show her who she belongs to."

Despite the lust burning through him, his brown eyes are flickering with appreciation and love. His lips turn up on one side in mischief. "Come on, you two. There'll be a test after. Better do a real good job and make Daddy proud."

Vale giggles and I let loose a snort.

"Daddy, huh?" I tease.

Vaughn shrugs, smirking. "We all have our kinks. Now move your asses. I don't want to have to get my belt."

"Now that's a kink I can't ignore," I jest as I rise with Vale in my arms. "Get upstairs and whip my ass so we can hurry and tag team your wife."

Vaughn's eyes flare with heat. "That mouth of yours does it to me every time."

When he starts prowling after us, Vale giggles and my heart thunders in my chest. This is where I belong. It's where I'll always belong. The glue. Holding both pieces of my heart together. And I'll never let go.

EPILOGUE

Vaughn
One year later...

The house is dark when I step inside. And quiet. Yawning, I set my messenger bag down and ignore the assignments that need grading. My not-so-willing student can help me grade that shit later. For now, though, I need to see my family. I stalk through the house and up the stairs. Bypassing our room, I head straight for the nursery. When I step inside, all the stress of the day melts away as I take in the scene. Aiden is asleep with his mouth hanging open as he sits in the glider, our son snuggled up against his chest.

They're fucking adorable.

I stare at Aiden, marveling at his strength. Somehow, he manages a husband and a wife, college, running the coffee shop full-time, and being a dad. Meanwhile, I can barely make it through a day on my own two feet. Even Vale is bedraggled and exhausted. But Aiden? He takes it all in with stride. Lifts the burdens on each of us when he feels it's too heavy. As Pastor McAvoy always says each Sunday, "God gives you miracles each day. What you do with them is up to you."

And Aiden is our miracle.

I walk into the room and take Logan from his arms. My son coos and it makes my chest squeeze with pride.

"We're going to have to hire him some help at the coffee shop," Vale whispers as she enters the room. Leah is nursing. As if he can sense it's feeding time, Logan wriggles in my grip.

"I agree. He needs a break," I utter as I walk over to her and kiss the top of her head. "And how are you, beautiful?"

She smiles up at me. "Perfect."

Leah's eyes are wide-open and she pulls from the breast letting milk run down her cheek as she smiles at me. So fucking cute.

"Hey, precious," I mutter, grinning at her.

She seeks out the breast once more and I wink

at Vale. When I turn from her, I find Aiden watching us. In the beginning of our relationship, he used to get a panicked look in his eyes. One that said he was afraid we'd leave him any minute. Now, he simply smiles when he sees us together. That fear has long been squashed.

He rises from his chair and stretches. "Logan had one helluva blowout earlier. Next one's all yours, Daddy."

I smirk. "Nah, I think you're pretty good at diaper duty."

Vale shakes her head. "Neither of you knows how to put the diaper back on right to save your lives. I swear I get peed on more times in a day I can count."

Aiden shrugs. "I can't be good at *everything*." He bends down and kisses Logan's forehead before giving me a quick kiss too. "How was class?

"Boring," I say with a snort.

Aiden beams at me. "Told you school sucks."

I roll my eyes but don't give him any shit. He works hard in college despite hating it. I know he wants to help Vale expand her business. They've even discussed changing it from just coffee to an actual restaurant. His focus on his business classes has become more intense and I couldn't be prouder.

Logan passes back out, so I set him in his crib. I admire my boy before looking over at his twin as she suckles my wife's breast. Twins. I'd nearly died from heart palpitations that day when Aiden and I crowded Vale as the technician told us we were having two babies rather than one. Where I was in shock and Vale was crying with happiness, Aiden simply reminded us that twins run in the family. Easton was right about those miracles. And our miracle helped give us two more.

"I'll get her to sleep. Aiden's about to crash. You don't look too far behind," Vale says, smiling. "I'll be there in a minute."

I wink at her before following Aiden down the hall. We've long since invested in a bigger bed. It gets hot when three people sleep together. By the time I reach our room, he's already down to his boxers and crawling into bed. I'm beat, so I undress to my boxers, then slide in beside him. My arm curls around him and I start to drift off. I wake when Vale joins us. She lies on his other side and threads her fingers with mine over his stomach.

"Love you guys," Vale says with a yawn.

"Love you too," Aiden and I both say.

We've all just drifted off when I hear one of the

babies crying. Despite being tired as hell, I slip out of the bed to go retrieve whichever one is fussing. Once inside the room, I look into Logan's crib. His crying stops when he sees me and his wide blue eyes regard me with such awe. I'll never get tired of the way my kids look at me. The way those babies' eyes light up when I enter the room.

I scoop my son in my arms and admire his perfect face.

He looks just like them.

Two people I love more than I can express.

"You just missed Daddy, didn't you?" I whisper, smiling at him. He smiles too and then I hear Leah fussing. It takes some finagling, but I manage to get her in my other arm. They both stare at me, cute as fucking hell.

Sitting in the glider, I admire both of their faces as I start telling them all about derivatives and the time value of money. If they're anything like their other daddy, they'll be asleep in no time.

Miracles.

Something tells me God has a few more in store.

Vale

Fourteen months later…

"Oh. My. God."

Logan beams at me. When he gives me that toothy grin, I can't even be mad at him. But boy oh boy is that child's a mess. And right now, he's both a figurative and literal mess.

"Snow!" he shrieks.

Leah runs around the corner and lets out a giggle. "Snow!"

"No," I admonish. "That's flour. Not snow. Oh my God."

Flour is everywhere. Logan managed to climb onto the counter, pull down a plastic tub of flour, and make a big damn mess with it.

He throws a handful of flour at his sister and she bursts into tears. When I realize I'm going to have to clean up this big mess, I start crying too. As soon as Logan understands he messed up, he begins wailing.

"Oh my babies," I sob, sitting down on the dusty floor. "Come here."

They run over to me and both try to cuddle in my lap. But there isn't much room. No, Aiden made sure of that when he knocked me up again with his super sperm.

With twins.

"Help me," I cry out to the heavens.

We're all three a sobbing mess when Aiden and Vaughn enter the kitchen. They've been out checking on a new property. The lease is up on the coffee shop and we're thinking there's no time like the present to start making the big changes we talked about.

"Holy shit," Aiden utters.

"Howee shit," Logan parrots and then reaches for his dad.

Aiden picks him up, smirking at his little copycat, and Vaughn takes Leah.

"Did Mommy make a mess?" Vaughn asks Leah.

Her bottom lip pokes out. "Logan make it snow."

Vaughn arches a brow at me and reaches a hand down. I grasp him and he helps me up. "Why don't you go rest and we'll take care of all this?"

"Really?" I ask, my lip trembling.

"Really," Aiden says, stepping to me to kiss my forehead. "I think Mommy need an N-A-P."

"Mommy does need a nap," I say with a sigh. Then, a fresh bout of tears washes over me. "How will I handle four?"

Vaughn chuckles. "Just like you handle

everything else. Like a boss. Plus, you have the two of us." He kisses her cheek. "Go wash up, babe, and take a break."

Both men are holding our children as though it's just another day in the Young household. Suddenly, I don't want to leave them. I don't want a break. I want to hold them all close and never let go.

"I sowwy, Mommy," Logan says, reaching for me.

My heart cracks open and I can't take it anymore. Even the hardest days are the best days. These people in this kitchen are my entire world.

"Aww," I coo, pulling him into my arms and kissing the top of his head. "It's okay, sweetie. I love you."

He gives me a sloppy toddler kiss.

Both Vaughn and Aiden are smirking at me.

"What?" I demand.

"You," Aiden says, grinning. "You're cute."

I feel anything but cute. I'm covered in flour now, I haven't showered, and I'm a snotty mess. Not to mention, I'm six months pregnant with more twins. I'm anything but cute.

"She doesn't believe it," Vaughn says, a wolfish grin on his face. "I think we're going to have to convince her later."

Aiden's smile is devilish. "Then I better get these

two cleaned up and ready for a N-A-P."

I narrow my eyes at them. "You can't convince me."

"You know we can," Vaughn says smugly.

Those two are cooking up something devious and I have a feeling it'll end up with the both of them feasting on my pussy later.

I suppose I like it when they convince me.

Aiden's eyes darken, easily reading my thoughts. He steals both kids from us, spins them around making them squeal, and then hollers over his shoulder. "Get her clean and ready. Daddy will be back in half an hour."

I wave my hand at the mess once he's gone. "And this?" I ask Vaughn.

"This can wait," he growls before pulling me to him. "But what we want to do to you won't. Let's get you showered, woman, because I'm hungry."

"Vaughn," I say, huffing, my cheeks reddening.

He winks at me. "Don't act like you aren't eager to feed your two favorite men in this world."

My thighs clench. Damn all these pregnancy hormones. Now that they're home and we're a team again, I'm feeling renewed and eager to spend some quality time with them. "Lead the way, lover."

Aiden

Five years later...

"Oh God," Vale whimpers against Vaughn's chest.

His brown eyes blaze with heat as he watches me. I love how intense he is sometimes. I grip my hard dick with my left hand and take a moment to admire the ring they bought me. We're not married as far as the law is concerned, but our bond is unbreakable. We have a family together and our love never wanes.

"You ready to take both your husbands' cocks?" I demand, slapping her curvy ass.

She groans. Vale fucking loves it when I refer to us as her husbands. "Yes," she moans a little too loudly.

"Keep our girl quiet," I instruct Vaughn. "Keep her pretty lips busy because I'm about to make her squeal."

They start kissing as I pour lube on my dick. I rub it in and then spread some on her asshole. Her hips rock back and forth as she rides Vaughn's dick. I toss the lube to the side and grip her hip with my free hand. Then, I slowly ease into my sweet Vale's ass. As always, she's tight, especially when he's inside her pussy. My eyes close as I push in. I love the way I can feel his dick just on the other side of her pussy walls. Once I'm deep inside her ass, I grip her hips and move her body to fuck us both. Her moans are loud, but she keeps getting silenced by his kisses.

Vaughn makes a sound of pleasure and our eyes meet. He kisses her, but his stare is on me. Together, we fuck her until she's shuddering with a wild orgasm. Vaughn's dick jolts and spasms inside her, which detonates me. I slide out of her ass and paint her pretty flesh with my cum. When I smear it across her ass, she lets out a scandalized huff.

"I like seeing my cum on you," I tell her with a shrug.

"I like seeing it too," Vaughn adds in agreement.

"I hate when you two tag team me," she grumbles.

Both Vaughn and I snort with laughter.

"What?" she huffs.

"We literally just tag teamed you and you did nothing but whimper and beg for it." I grin as she climbs off Vaughn and pouts. "Admit it, beautiful."

Her lips twitch. "Fine, I love it."

"That a girl," Vaugh says, grinning as we head for the shower.

We end up getting frisky in the shower, but I slip

out of the spray when my daddy senses alert me to the fact that one of our kids is awake. I quickly dry off and throw on some clothes before opening the bedroom door.

Leah stands in the hallway rubbing her eyes with one hand and holding her little sister Ember's hand.

"What's wrong?" I ask, kneeling on the carpet in front of them.

"Ember had a nightmare," Leah says.

I scoop up Ember and walk them back to their room. Leah is a good big sister to the girls. Once inside their room, I smile to see Eliza sprawled out in her twin bed still snoring logs. Sleeps crazy just like her mom.

"Night, Daddy," Leah says, hugging my thigh before climbing back on the top bunk that's situated across from Eliza's bed.

"Night, my beautiful girl."

She beams at me and crawls under her covers.

Ember tugs my hand. She's our silent girl. Where Eliza will blab your ear off about everything, Ember is reserved and quiet. I know she can speak, though, because when she doesn't think we notice, I catch her singing to her baby brother Jace.

"Come on," I tell her. "I'm sleepy. Got room in

your bed for me?"

Ember nods, smiling. We squish together on the bottom bunk and I inhale her hair. I love my kids. Who knew that one day I'd have five of them? Now I get why Dad is always so stupid happy. Kids will do that to you.

Years ago if I tried to imagine my future, I would have hoped it would be this. Happy with Vaughn and Vale with a litter of kids to love. I wouldn't have imagined we could make something like this work. But we do. And we do it well. It takes everyone doing their part to make it all successful.

I squeeze my daughter and she whispers, "I wuv you, Daddy."

My heart clenches.

"Love you too, angel."

Everyone has their parts in this family.

Vaughn is the fierce leader. The strength and the resilience. Vale is the love and laughter and sweetness. Our children are the lights, scaring away darkness forever. Together, we're a team.

As for me?

I hold them all tightly together because I'm the glue.

And I'm never letting go.

The End

If you loved Aiden in *The Glue*,
you'll love his twin brother's story in *Lawn Boys*!

K Webster's Taboo World
Cast of Characters

Brandt Smith (Rick's Best Friend)
Kelsey McMahon (Rick's Daughter)
Rick McMahon (Sheriff)
Mandy Halston (Kelsey's Best Friend)

Miles Reynolds (Drew's Best Friend)
Olivia Rowe (Max's Daughter/Sophia's Sister)

Dane Alexander (Max's Best Friend)
Nick Stratton

Judge Maximillian "Max" Rowe (Olivia and Sophia's Father)
Dorian Dresser

Drew Hamilton (Miles's Best Friend)
Sophia Rowe (Max's Daughter/Olivia's Sister)

Easton McAvoy (Preacher)
Lacy Greenwood (Stephanie's Daughter)

Stephanie Greenwood (Lacy's Mother)
Anthony Blakely (Quinn's Son)
Aiden Blakely (Quinn's Son)

Quinn Blakely (Anthony and Aiden's Father)
Ava Prince (Lacy/Raven/Olivia's friend)

Karelma Bonilla (Mateo's Daughter)
Adam Renner (Principal)

Coach Everett Long (Adam's friend)
River Banks (Olivia's Best Friend)

Mateo Bonilla (Four Fathers Series Side Character)

Vaughn Young
Vale Young

K Webster's Taboo World Reading List

These don't necessarily have to be read in order to enjoy, but if you would like to know the order I wrote them in, it is as follows (with more being added to as I publish):

Bad Bad Bad
Coach Long
Ex-Rated Attraction
Mr. Blakely
Malfeasance
Easton (Formerly known as Preach)
Crybaby
Lawn Boys
Renner's Rules
The Glue

Books by K Webster

ACKNOWLEDGEMENTS

Thank you to my husband. You're my biggest supporter and my inspiration. I love you so much!

A huge thank you to my Krazy for K Webster's Books reader group. You all are insanely supportive and I can't thank you enough.

A gigantic thank you to those who always help me out. Elizabeth Clinton, Ella Stewart, Misty Walker, Holly Sparks, Jillian Ruize, Gina Behrends, and Nikki Ash—you ladies are my rock!

A special thanks to Misty Walker for always being there. Through thick and thin. At a moment's notice. For knowing exactly what I need, exactly when I need it. You're more than a life saver, you're the best friend a girl could ask for. I would hug you, but I hope you can settle with me petting you with my broom from afar. Love you, boo!

A big thank you to my author friends who have given me your friendship and your support. You have no idea how much that means to me.

Thank you to all of my blogger friends both big and small that go above and beyond to always share my stuff. You all rock! #AllBlogsMatter

Emily A. Lawrence, thank you SO much for editing this book. You're a rock star and I can't thank you enough! Love you!

Thank you Stacey Blake for being amazing as always when formatting my books and in general. I love you! I love you! I love you!

A big thanks to my PR gal, Nicole Blanchard. You are fabulous at what you do and keep me on track!

Lastly but certainly not least of all, thank you to all of the wonderful readers out there who are willing to hear my story and enjoy my characters like I do. It means the world to me!

ABOUT THE AUTHOR

K Webster is the *USA Today* bestselling author of over fifty romance books in many different genres including contemporary romance, historical romance, paranormal romance, dark romance, romantic suspense, taboo romance, and erotic romance. When not spending time with her hilarious and handsome husband and two adorable children, she's active on social media connecting with her readers.

Her other passions besides writing include reading and graphic design. K can always be found in front of her computer chasing her next idea and taking action. She looks forward to the day when she will see one of her titles on the big screen.

Join K Webster's newsletter to receive a couple of updates a month on new releases and exclusive content. To join, all you need to do is go here (www.authorkwebster.com).

Facebook:
www.facebook.com/authorkwebster

Blog:
authorkwebster.wordpress.com

Twitter:
twitter.com/KristiWebster

Email:
kristi@authorkwebster.com

Goodreads:
www.goodreads.com/user/show/10439773-k-webster

Instagram:
instagram.com/kristiwebster

K WEBSTER'S
Taboo World

two interconnected stories

BAD
BAD
BAD

two taboo treats

k webster

Bad Bad Bad

Two interconnected stories. Two taboo treats.

Brandt's Cherry Girl

He's old enough to be her father.
She's his best friend's daughter.
Their connection is off the charts.
And so very, very wrong.
This can't happen.
Oh, but it already is…

Sheriff's Bad Girl

He's the law and follows the rules.
She's wild and out of control.
His daughter's best friend is trouble.
And he wants to punish her…
With his teeth.

USA TODAY BESTSELLING AUTHOR
K WEBSTER

She's a hurdle in his way...
and he wants to jump her.

a taboo treat

COACH
LONG

Coach Long

Coach Everett Long has a chip on his shoulder.
Working every day with the man who stole his
fiancée leaves him pissed and on edge.
His temper is volatile and his attitude sucks.

River Banks is a funky-styled runner
with a bizarre past.
Starting over at a new school was supposed to
be easy…but she should have known better.
She likes to antagonize and tends to go after
what she's not supposed to have.

When the arrogant bully meets the strong-willed
brat, it sparks an illicit attraction.
Together, they heat up the track with
longing and desire.
Everything about their chemistry is wrong.
So why does it feel so right?

She's a hurdle in his way and, dear God does
he want to jump her.
Will she be worth the risk or
will he fall flat on his face?

Ex-Rated Attraction

I liked Caleb.

I like his dad more.

Miles Reynolds sent shocks through me the very first time I met him. With his full beard and sculpted ass, he's every inch a heroic, powerful Greek god.

He saved me from a bad situation and now he's all I can think of. Every minute of every hour of every day, I want that man.

He's warned me away, says I can't handle what he has to give.

But I know better.

Miles is exactly what I need—now, then and forever.

Mr. Blakely

It started as a job.

It turned into so much more.

Mr. Blakely is strict with his sons, but he's soft and gentle with me.

The powerful businessman is something else entirely when we're together.

Boss, teacher, lover…husband.

My hopes and dreams for the future have changed. I want—no, I need—him by my side.

a taboo treat

malfeasance

Judge Rowe
never had
a problem with
morality...
until her.

K WEBSTER

Malfeasance

Max Rowe always follows the rules.
A successful judge.
A single father.
A leader in the community.
Doing the right thing means everything.

But when he finds himself rescuing an incredibly
young woman,
everything he's worked hard for is quickly forgotten.
The only thing that matters is keeping her safe.
She's gorgeous, intelligent, and the ultimate
temptation.
Doing the wrong thing suddenly feels right.

Their chemistry is intense.
It's a romance no one will approve of, yet one they
can't ignore.
Hot, fast, and explosive.
Someone is going to get burned.

He'll give up everything for her...
because without her, he is nothing.

EASTON

K WEBSTER

Easton

A man who made countless mistakes.
A woman with a messy past.

He's tasked with helping her find her way.
She's lost in grief and self-doubt.

Together they begin something innocent…
Until it's not.

His freedom is at risk.
Her heart won't survive another break.

All rational thinking says they
should stay away from each other.
But neither are very good
at following the rules.

A deep, dark craving.
An overwhelming need.
A burn much hotter than any hell
they could ever be condemned to.

He'll give up everything for her…
because without her, he is nothing.

He likes her screams.
He likes them an awful lot.
Crybaby
a taboo treat
K WEBSTER

Crybaby

Stubborn.
Mouthy.
Brazen.
Two people with vicious tongues.
A desperate temptation neither can ignore.

An injury has changed her entire life.
She's crippled, hopeless, and angry.
And the only one who can lessen her pain is him.

Being the boss is sometimes a pain in the ass.
He's irritated, impatient, and doesn't play games.
Yet he's the only one willing to fight her…for her.

Daring.
Forbidden.
Out of control.
Someone is going to get hurt.
And, oh, how painfully sweet that will be.

The grass is greener where
he points his hose...

lawn
BOYS
a taboo treat

USA TODAY BESTSELLING AUTHOR
K WEBSTER

Lawn Boys

She's lived her life and it has been a good one.
Marriage. College. A family.
Slowly, though, life moved forward and left her at a
standstill.

Until the lawn boy barges into her world.
Bossy. Big. Sexy as hell.
A virile young male to remind her she's all woman.

Too bad she's twice his age.
Too bad he doesn't care.

She's older and wiser and more mature.
Which means absolutely nothing when he's invading
her space.

USA TODAY BESTSELLING AUTHOR
K WEBSTER

Principal Renner,
I've been *bad.*
Again.

a taboo treat

RENNER'S
Rules

Renner's Rules

I'm a bad girl.
I was sent away.
New house. New rules. New school.
Change was supposed to be…good.

Until I met him.

No one warned me Principal Renner would be so
hot.
I'd expected some old, graying man in a brown suit.
Not this.
Not well over six feet of lean muscle and piercing
green eyes.
Not a rugged-faced, ax-wielding lumberjack of a
man.

He's grouchy and rude and likes to boss me around.
I find myself getting in trouble just so he'll punish
me.
Especially with his favorite metal ruler.

Being bad never felt so good

Made in the USA
San Bernardino, CA
05 September 2018